MW01134323

Bust It Like A Mule

The Tale of Cotton Kingfisher

by

Caleb Mannan

Cover art 'Cotton' by Caleb Mannan

Copyright 2015 Caleb Joshua Mannan

I'd like to thank my wife editor creativepartner *Bust It* musical collaborator big sky girl Jenny Anne, who made this book possible. Babe, I aint nothin on a stick without you.

To my brother artist partner Kevin Morgan - Cotton Kingfisher would not be if it wasn't for some of your cuss and song characters like Rhubarb Tweady and Alligator. Brother Jacob Mannan, thank you for always believing in me, you are my Comanche. Thanks to all my brothers and sisters who read for me, listen to me, put up with me, and still treat me as sane.

Lastly (but certainly not leastly), much affection to Miller High Life, Tanqueray Gin and black coffee.

In the spirit of my Okie grandpa JE Jones

1.

He was an ornery mean cuss that was ox bow strong and mule kick tough and he didn't care if he won or lost as long as he was fightin. No one could say Cotton Kingfisher didn't live life like he meant it though one couldn't say exactly what he meant when he was living it just that he sure as hell meant it. He had a fire in his belly like a potbellied stove glowing and that fire licked out at times and consumed those around him I guess you could say. He'd break a fist and keep right on fighting he'd love a woman and keep right on leaving he'd fall over dead and keep right on drinkin he lost his driving license but kept right on driving. He was a man's man that none of the men liked that's how goddamn rough and tumble he was and may God strike me dead if I tell a lie.

Being that Cotton was such a cuss no one'd think that a woman would cotton to him no pun intended but he got all the ladies he liked and more not the kind you take home to momma of course but barflies and floozies and burlesquies are women too and some of them are damn beautiful enough to break a man's heart but Cotton's heart had never been broke because he wasn't jackass enough to hand it over to any one woman or all of the above for that matter so he kept wham bamming and thank you ma'ming from the South clean up into the West.

When he first started to wander like Cain roaming over the face of the earth he figured he had but a few choices as to which way to go. In the 30's he was still in Oklahoma the place of his birth and things was dead and dying there at the time like a horse taken out to pasture so he knew he was already as far South as he wanted to go this side of hell. He could go North or East but those places were filled with damn Yankees that thought they were somethin on a stick and bygod they weren't nothin on a stick but shit. Then there was the West with all its wide open country and cowboys and Indians real Indians like the kind you see in the movies not some drunk ass old chief wearing white man's clothes beggin for pennies outside in the street until the cops came and busted him and it busted your heart to see no real Indians bygod.

When he left home he was just a kid so his Okie accent had kind of faded to a lazy blur by now but it came roaring back when he was angry and somehow he was always angry so it was always roaring back and people knew he was a Johnny Reb straight off and he caught shit for it out West whether they like to say that or not he just did and I don't know what this says about the States but Cotton was mean enough to take on the whole West bygod and he did from the Dakotas to California and Oregon and Washington and Wyoming and Montana and even New Mexico and Arizone raising cane and hell all the while.

So Cotton headed out West just like all young men do at some point or wish they did or hell they should because the West is best the place where the Johnny Reb and the Damn Yank meet together in a lawless frontier of pioneering spirit and manifest destiny nestled between the bouncing breasts of Lady Liberty's National Parks leastaways this is what Cotton thought and he aimed to prove it or at least to find out.

He rode the rails a hell ton as well as he went by way of his thumb a big thumb bygod hitchin it on the American highway that was cutting concrete stretchmarks across the belly of the states. Cotton had a big bygod thumb for when he was younger he was working on a farm in Nevada of all places and they were laying down a cattle guard that was so goddamn heavy they had to carry it with hay hooks and lift and walk a pace then set it down and lift and walk a pace and set it down and lift and walk a pace and set it down over and over until they got to where it was supposed to go and they were laying it in place and Cotton told em to hold it steady while he set it in place and they didn't hold it steady they dropped it and a good goddamn three hundred pounds or more squished his thumb flat. All Cotton could do was nothin for it hurt so bad until he finally hollered for em to get the goddamn monkey sucker thing off with a bunch of other words those men had never even heard and I bet those curse words're still smudging up the Nevada sky. They did lift the thing off finally and I don't know if they did it on purpose for Cotton bein a cuss and all or if it was an accident but Cotton thought they did it on purpose and a lot more than them men's thumbs was flat when he got done with them and he had to leave Nevada straight away.

I don't exactly know all where Cotton went in those years sometimes staying in one place longer than others and maybe shacking up with a pretty girl or two but he had spent more years wandering than not by the time this story takes place and he wasn't young anymore like he used to be. His once easy rollin ways had turned to more like a creaking iron switch track lever being thrown every time he moved on maybe not in his soul but in his bones because his bones'd been wandering like a skeleton out of the closet for quite a piece now and them bones I'd wager was tired but I guess that's bound to happen when you get a start like Cotton and keep on goin and this is how Cotton got started and kept on goin.

He got the stuffing kicked out of him no pun intended by his daddy when he was a boy and he got sick of it so he lit out when he was just a kid though he had nowhere to go. He got robbed by a bunch of hobos on his first ride West and they woulda sodomized him he heard them telling each other over the fire aside the railroad tracks but Cotton wouldn't have none of that and when they came at him thinking he was sleeping he rolled over and slashed open one of them's faces with a broken piece of glass and he kept right on slashing and he killed one of them bygod. He was just thirteen at the time and he was never sodomized nor none tried thereafter bygod. He stoked up the hobo fire aside the tracks and threw the dead body he killed in it and some of the others watched him do this as they moaned over their glass slashed gashes and Cotton said to them

"I could kill y'all right now but I'll spare y'all cause I am just a boy yet"

and he meant it and those men had never heard such talk nor seen such things from but a boy.

Cotton missed his family but he never saw them again once he left and maybe it was just as well for he couldn't take his momma's dog sad eyes with a baby suckling at her bosom no more though those eyes came back to haunt him as a grown man especially after he heard many years ago she succumbed to hardship and was buried somewhere in the old hills of Oklahoma wherein he used to roam hiding out from his daddy. He guessed he missed his momma he didn't rightly know but it's hard to miss something when you don't know what it is and you and I both know it bygod.

So here he was now the toughest railrider to ever grace the iron python and all the men respected and feared him clean from his days as but a boy yet when he killed that damn hobo who had tried to take advantage of him furthered by his reputation as a fierce ass brawler and mean old mule strong cuss who was rougher than a cob. Tales live long on the rails like whispered mythologies over late night star

13

fires and in musty hay coal box cars sheltered from the rain and the mythologies of Cotton was long and far and many. He had some men that tried to follow him like the Apostles followed Jesus but Cotton was no fisher of bygod men so he eventually managed to shake them so he could drink in solitude and listen to the whistle by the tracks and wander over open fields and look for Indians like he had since he was a boy. It always bothered him how he never saw many Indians out West not like he had thought he would as a boy he guessed it was the same as Oklahoma but he thought to see them with their feathers and robes and such when he had first come out West as a boy. Once in Seattle he had seen some injuns off of their land the government had give em or held em to and they had their hair cut like white men but Cotton could tell by their wild eyes they hadn't been tamed and he went up to them and said

"You lost your land and your homes and now your hair"

and one of them Indians says

"We lost our path"

and this made Cotton heartsick though he told himself it was just gut burn from the rotgut wine he was drinking but you and I know what that burn came from was a sick heart by what the Indian had said about losing their path.

Cotton left Seattle by the Sea after that and never returned though he had to agree it was one of the most beautiful cities he'd ever seen by the inlet of the

Ocean ringed with great god mountains and pines. He didn't care much for the rain though always constantly misting down on you like God was cryin because it rained so much even He got the blues. On the sunny days in Seattle Cotton figured that this must be what Michael rowed his boat ashore for but that was just on sunny days and he was glad to leave the rain and his short order cook job that he was about to lose because he had thrown a plate at an ornery cuss customer who said his steak was too well done and broke the poor bastard's nose who was a banker and was likely to sue Cotton for all he had which he didn't know was nothin and bring the police down on him so he left.

He rode the shaking sooty beast out of Washington and into Idaho where he got into a ruckus with some foreign fruit pickers who to his reputation did not proceed and they quarreled. Cotton couldn't understand a cottonpicking word that came out of their goddamn mouths even though he had worked with many foreign migrant workers he took pride in not understanding them but he didn't like the looks of them just the same and there was fifteen or twenty of em to his one and they wanted his rucksack on his back over some misunderstanding for he was being a surly cuss and he said to them

"Go get in bed with your momma"

and though none of them understood exactly what he said they understood the gesture that proceeded it from him and they came at him all at once and Cotton stood like a tree in a storm like Samson amongst the Philistines as they rushed around him and he brought his knotty pine ox strong limbs down upon them and broke a few skulls and busted some arms and legs and noses and his own nose got broke bygod and his brow bled like hell but he beat them lean mean pickers down by sheer bygod determination and righteous rage and eventually the ones that were still standing fled like the Egyptians fled when the Red Sea came crashing in on them but in that Bible story the Red Sea wave swallowed all the Egytipans whether they ran or not and it was the same with those fleeing fruit pickers and the Red Sea crashing wave that was Cotton Kingfisher.

Cotton was left alone with a bunch of bodies around him like he was that ol prophet whatshisname standing in the valley of dry bones and for the first time in his life he felt tore up and broke up and tired. The train rattled his bones hard and the soot settled in his lungs heavy and the blood coagulated on his face and he felt all shook up and like the earth was tryin to kill him and he don't know how to make the earth happy. For the first time in his life Cotton felt lost real lost truly lost like he suddenly missed home when he'd never had one in the first place and he wasn't sure why and even if he was sure why it wouldn't do him no damn good because he had no home to go back to.

So after Idaho Cotton hopped off the rails in Montana looking for something that he wasn't sure existed but he bygod was going to look for it and that thing he was lookin for was home or a rough approximation thereof I suppose.

2.

"Where the hell am I goin"

Cotton asked the attendant at the filling station where he wandered to off the rails in Montana and the boy just stared back at his blood crusted mug and says

"Mister are you ok?"

"Hell yeah son where am I goin"

Cotton goes on lighting a smoke and the kid said

"Well that depends on where you're headed."

"I wanna see some cottonpickin Indians not the broke ass kind that wear white man's clothes but the kind that have feathers in their hair n robes and such."

The boy attendant pushed his cap back on his head and scratched a bit and thought and finally he says

"Well you can always go up to Glacier National Park and I think they have some of the Indians come down all in get up."

"Is it a smoke and mirrors get up or a real get up?"

"Well I guess I don't know mister. Just that they wear feathers and colorful blankets and such. The Blackfeet is up thataway."

Cotton'd heard of the Blackfeet and liked the sound of them though he wasn't sure what being of blackfeet meant so he decided to follow that kid's finger pointing up North past some mountains. He washed himself up right in the filling station washroom with the travelers giving him dirty stares on account of he looked like he had been drug through a knothole backwards and him not giving a damn well maybe just a little but only on account of his new feeling of sensitiveness in regards to the earth having it out for him. Then he hefted his Army Navy rucksack and headed up into the meaty part of the big sky country just west of where the Rocky Mountains jut up like a prehistoric crusty ol spine and cut off the plains from the rest of the West. It was slow goin up the road because no one was stopping for a stiff walking scarred up rucksack wearin stranger even though it was the summer and summer is the time when the place was alive with tourists come to see Glacier Park up North where Cotton was headed. He gave up even havin his thumb hung out like a tired old dog's tongue and went off the road a piece and built a fire and cooked himself a can a beans and drank from an old Army canteen.

Now the thing about Cotton is he was a wanderer

but he wasn't no dadblamed bum or beggar. He took care of hisself bygod and can't no man say different because he did and that's the Gospel truth. He worked for what he bought when he worked and when he bought and he was proud of this being he was a bindlestiff not into piddlin. Once a man in a fancy hat gave Cotton some change on account of Cotton looked like a bum in his knapsack and all and Cotton threw that change back in fancy hat's face bygod being that he was not a bum he was a hobo. You see there is a difference from a hobo and a bum and the difference is that a hobo chooses the life of the gypsy and he earns his way in it while the bum just finds the wandering life like a leaf blown in the wind without purpose and he's got no shame in beggin. Not Cotton Kingfisher bygod you'd never met a prouder man than he and if you caught him beggin youda caught him dead because I aint never seen it and aint no one ever else and if they tell you different they are liars. But no one'd tell you different because the tales of Cotton still run strong and long along the rails like the whistle in the wind.

Another thing about Cotton as we see him settin there off in the pines cooking his can a beans out of the big sky big sun is that he was mighty generous even if he didn't want people to know that he was. He'd give you the shirt off his back if you were cold and don't let any man tell you different not even Cotton. He gave away cans of beans and ears of corn and field rabbits and scrounged grouse and even the leftovers of a venison he said he caught with his bare hands though no one believed him but was too scared to tell him that no he did not. He gave a black man all his cash once and he gave an Indian back his blanket when the Indian lost it to Cotton in a drunken bet and he said to this Indian

"Now who's the Indian giver"

and they got along fine after that.

But he earned what he owned is what I am tryin to say to you though little it was like that Army Navy rucksack and that can a beans he is eating right there in the Montana sun and those railroad worker pants and those redwing boots and those t shirts and those denim jackets and flannel shirts and the wool bedroll that the Indian gave him back after Cotton had given it back to him after he'd lost it fair and square to Cotton in a drunken bet. Even the railroad engineer cap he wears when it gets hotter than Old Blickeys he got fair and square jawed. He got that there hat one of his most prized possessions from a hoghead which is what the hobos call a rail engineer who had grown real fond of Cotton through all his rail ridin years and refused to let anyone throw Cotton off the train and that agreement still goes on as long as the length of the track from Seattle down to New Mexico though the last I heard that hoghead is dead and gone God rest his soul.

Cotton took his time eatin his beans right out of the can heated in the coals and he listened to a murder of crows in a gaggle of trees calling him bad names even though he is awful fond of the blackburned birds himself as he sees them as his angels that follow him wherever he goes no matter what they caw otherwise. Then he rolled out his wool blanket and fell asleep beside the fire every now and again hearing a car rush past but not caring because he was too wore out to go catch it with his thumb like a dog running down a meal cart.

He slept in peace without all the aches left over from his heartbreaking fight and he dreamt but he wished he wouldn't because he had the dream he always had of his daddy and the dream goes like this but it aint really a dream just a retelling of a tale from Cotton's past played on the back of his eyelids-

Cotton's daddy wasn't a nice man and a lousy cuss drunk to boot but he liked to play music on the guitar and sing and Cotton had never heard anything so beautiful as when his daddy would play and sing even if he had to listen outside the shack because he didn't want to stir up his daddy's violent tendencies towards the boy the boy being himself. Cotton's heart would be filled up with strange stirrings as if angels themselves were singing those country and western songs his daddy was singing in that high Okie voice of his and he would just sit and listen outside the shack.

One time right before Cotton fled from the Oklahoma hills forever his daddy laid into him good and liked to break his nose hadn't his momma pulled his old man off of him and then his daddy lit into her until Cotton grabbed a piece of firewood and hit his daddy's skull so hard he coldcocked the mean old sonofabitch. Now Cotton's momma stood up smoothin out her threadbare dress like nothing had just occurred though Cotton had seen it occur with his own two eyes and could see her bleeding from the mouth and nose with his own two eyes. They say this is where Cotton's legendary rage comes is when he sees his momma standing there bleeding and smiling eyes darting like a scared rabbit and a bleeding trickle from the lip and nose. I can't say for sure because I think Cotton had the rage before that and I wager one has to have the rage to survive a daddy like that but whatever the case may be he went and got his daddy's guitar and he went and he busted it right over his daddy's passed out noggin and he kept beating and beating until his momma pulled him off and his daddy's head was flowing blood and that guitar was a splintered mess of a wreck then he went and hid up in a tree. He expected his daddy to come out roaring after him into the cicada humid night but night fell and all he heard from the house was his daddy weepin when his daddy saw that his guitar was all busted up because they were dirt broke poor and guitars were like gold. Cotton sat up in that tree hiding out from his daddy hearing him in the house cryin and he felt so sad all over because his daddy was sad even though his daddy was the devil. This is when Cotton knew he would never hear his daddy sing nor play ever again and this is when he lit out for the West and never looked back.

But all that to say that Cotton would dream about this incident from time to time and he dreamt it now as he slept there in the pines under the big sky beside the road to Glacier Park on his bedroll that the Indian had give back to him that blanket being one of his most favorite things.

3·

Cotton got up the next morning and stretched feeling a mite better though his nose sounded like a rusty muffler and his bones creaked like them pines in the wind. The crows were gone now and the fire was out and Cotton followed the road up a piece and he began to feel a bit of iron fall outta his step until he was whistlin in the sun like a regular goddamn Johnny Appleseed though he had no trees to plant nor reason to plant them. He made it quite a few miles up the road and saw the rail tracks running along the Clark Fork River so he made camp and hoped to catch the rails further up into the meaty part of Montana. He made himself a fine camp for he had no idea how long he would have to wait for the next train and he figured if it showed too soon to make all his work on his camp for not he could just wave it on and catch the next train that was the beauty of Cotton's life and the beauty of Montana.

He dug into his ruck and found him some fishing twine and fishing barbs wrapped around an Oregon yew stick that he'd got from the Oregon Coast as a walking stick until it broke over some nimrod's skull and he cast out into the Clark Fork River looking for a bite for lunch.

While he's out there fishin we can rifle though his bag right quick and you can see that Cotton aint no thief or bum or beggar or louse as he's got the possessions that most men have only he don't have too many of them like most men or the trappings therewith to hang them in.

He had some hair cream for his glossy pompadour that he didn't like mussed and this is the reason that he didn't wear his engineer cap that the old hoghead who is dead God rest his soul give him all that much although it is one of his prize possessions for when the sun was beating down upon his brow or when he's fishin like he is now so the hat is with him pulled low to cut the sun's sparkle glare off the river. He had an old pigsticker that looked like he had procured it from a Leatherneck in an Indian leg wrasslin match or maybe he was telling the truth and he earned that knife by serving Uncle Sam during the War as he was old enough to have been in the War of course though he seems ageless and on cold nights you think you can spot a small hitch in his giddyup if you squint real tight that may be from grenade shrapnel or a Jap bullet but he's only ever said that once or so when he had too much whiskey I was told about the knife and bein in the War so maybe it is none of my business. No one could say either way and no one sure as hell wasn't going to call him a liar at least not in the presence of forementioned pigsticker well hell I guess just not at all knife or no for Cotton is a mean buck cuss. He didn't wear the knife on his belt no more like he used to wear a knife on his belt in the old days cause it just called attention to himself and he'd rather not as he got older and he didn't care for run ins with cops and railyard bulls like he had in the old days just for a scrap and sides he didn't need to wear no goddamn knife for men didn't mess with him none. All the bulls on the railways never bothered Cotton none now for it just wasn't worth losing an arm or a leg or an eye and so he just put the knife in his bag on his back. In that rucksack he also had matches and extra t shirts and socks and drawers and a few jackets and the Indian blanket attached to the bottom proper and an army mess kit complete with steel utensils and an army canteen and canned goods and a tobacco tin with cigarette makins and other odds n ends and maybe some things that Cotton has hidden away. But he had bought these all with his own cash that he earned from cooking or the Forest Service crew or bucking bales or picking fruit or delivering advertisements or working the docks or working in a mill or just tough hard ass labor which Cotton was accustomed to on account of his daddy always tellin him that it was a tough row to hoe so you had to bust it like a mule and he did. There's no cash in the bag for Cotton kept his cash if he had any in his sock under his beat up smooth worn boots on account of gettin robbed by the hobos on his first ride West when they rifled his pack cottonpickin beggars and looters and thieves with no goddamn class.

He was fishin there on the smooth rollin Clark Fork

River when he heard something along the bank behind him and thinking it was someone come to steal his rucksack and all his earthly possessions he turned real quicklike and he saw a boy watching him it was an Indian boy and he came down to Cotton and said

"You can't fish here"

and Cotton replied

"The hell I can't"

"Are you Indian?"

the boy asked.

"This is as dark as I'll ever get"

Cotton replies meaning no.

"Then you can't fish here. This is Indian land."

"All this land they gave to you injuns"

Cotton says lookin about at the river and the beautiful banks and the trees and the mountains and he has seen some Indian land and it sure as hell don't look like this.

"I guess."

"Well don't that beat a hen awormin"

Cotton hollers which is about as clear as mud to the Indian boy and me as well for that matter though by the way he hollers it he means he'll be damned.

"You don't talk like no injun"

says Cotton and the boy does not know what that means neither for Indians just speak like everybody else don't they but Cotton is just staring at him so he replies

"We all go to school."

"Even I didn't go to school now injuns are what's this world comin to? What'd ya say if I told you that I was gonna fish here anyhow"

"I'd tell you that the police will probably come and take you away."

"Well for Pete's sake aint that a fine kettle a fish! Damn me gently I just want to eat is all! All this land gettin cut up like a side of beef with all the fencesandzonesandcountiesandrezsandsuch it's a bygod cryin shame"

and the boy said nothing.

"Well fine then you smartass I will just starve thanks to you"

Cotton said as he reeled in his line.

"You don't have to starve" the boy said "we have food at our house."

"I'll be a monkey's uncle" Cotton said "Why didn't you say so in the first place"

and Cotton followed the boy feeling like Montana really was the place for him to be.

The boy took Cotton to his home and the Indian family wasn't in colorful blankets nor feathers in their hair but they wore denim jeans and flannel shirts and their hair was long so Cotton figured this was about as good as it could get. He was excited to see what an Indian family would be eating whether it be trout or venison or maybe bison or rabbit but come to find out it was goddamned canned beans just like Cotton had in his bag though they made a cornpone that was good but on the dry side so it needed molasses and they didn't have none. But Cotton figured this was the first time he had dined with a Native family and he felt a part of something though they ate in silence and did not speak to him and neither he them. The Indian father came home late and he had cheap cans of beer and I will be jiggered if he did not share them with Cotton while the children played outside with the dogs.

"Where are you going?"

the Indian father asked of him.

"I aint rightly sure"

Cotton replied after a swig of beer

"I guess I'll see it when it sees me I fancy myself goin on up to Glacier Park to take a peek at them mountains."

The Indian father nodded and says

"The Land Where the World Began"

"Is that what they say"

Cotton asks and Indian father takes a drink of his beer then goes

28

"It is what we say."

"Well then I guess it is a good place for a man who
don't know where he belongs now aint it"

and Cotton would not have said this to just anybody
but he felt the Indian father understood especially
after the way he had said The Land Where the World
Began. The Indian father nodded and Cotton could
tell that indeed the Indian father did understand.

Cotton stayed on with the Indian family a few days
happier n a hog on ice just camping out front of
their trailer by a fire under the big sky big stars and
playing with the children and the dogs and drinking
beer with Indian father. As I said before he was no
bum or beggar so he worked for his food and beer
by helping Indian Father push some rusty hunks of
junks of cars off the property over a ledge while the
children watched with serious faces for they saw
Cotton was strong as a bygod bear for he did not
need Indian Father to help him lug those cars he
just got behind them and shoved them off the cliff
himself so as Indian Father would turn and the job
would be done and he would shake his head for he
had never seen a stronger man nor a white man ever
helped him as much. Cotton stayed on like this until
he felt bad that he was eatin the injun family out of
house and home and drinking all their beer though
he worked for it for this is just the kind of man he
is so he said he must be headed out even though he
really didn't want to because he liked that family
very much and began to wish it was his own but he
also knew this was the biggest reason of all for an
old broke down hobo like himself to get a move on

so he did.

4.

The Indian family knew another Indian family that had a broke down old truck and they hitched Cotton a ride up to the nearest town Cotton being in the back of the truck with all the kids and dogs to see him off and Indian father ridin shotgun for Cotton would not take the seat when Indian Father offered it to him. They took him quite a piece up the river and out of Indian land and when they dropped him at the filling station Indian Father asked of him

"What will you do now?"

and Cotton said

"Bust it like a mule"

then they shook hands through the truck window and all the kids waved and the dogs barked then Cotton started walking and he kept on walking until he reached another broke down jerkwater town with a shabby main street and an economy about the size of the blade of grass tween Cotton's teeth. Now by about this time he was tired and his feet were sore and it was hotter than Ol Blickey's under the big sky big sun so Cotton decided he needed a cold beer or a hot cup of joe but he couldn't decide which because he craved a frosty longneck real bad but he also liked his hot cup of joe and he had learned from the Mexicans who he picked fruit with that if it is hot you drink coffee because it regulates your bodily temperature or some such thing or other and he believed it for them Mexicans they sure as hell knew about the bygod heat. So he stopped in for a hot cup of joe and some cold water in a little café place even though the locals looked at him sidewayslike and he didn't care none. He liked Montana and he thought Montana liked him and no one could tell him different because that's just the way that man was. While he was sittin sipping his joe his mind rolled back like an old musty rug out of the attic to the door of that old homestead in the hills with his momma's sad eyes and his daddy's eerie guitar broke wailin and to his little brother and his little sisters who were just real little when he left. Being that Cotton was a free spirit he didn't mind leaving his family and never lookin back but being that he was a man of flesh and blood he never forgot nor forgave himself that he left his family and never looked back not on account of his daddy and maybe just a little bit on account of his poor momma but mainly due to his baby brother and sisters. Some nights he'd have terrible dreams about them and wake up screamin and all the other's around him in the train yard would scatter like mice because they thought the tomcat was powerful angry and he was but not at them mice just at himself and his daddy and maybe his momma a bit and maybe even though it pains me to say this and I take my hat off as I do the Good Lord Up Above. Whenever you see a man thats angry at the hole in him you know that that man is angry with God for that hole in him is where the Holy Spirit sets or don't if you get my meaning. Now I aint sayin Cotton was a damnation in the spiritual sense no bygod not me I'd never say that about Cotton he was a goddamn Saint but I am sayin all this just to let you know about Cotton and his innards the good and the bad so I told you that.

So he sat there drinkin his coffee and thinkin on his little ones and he wondered what they were up to these days and where they were and he wouldn't even know if they was dead or alive especially his little brother since after the War cause his baby brother was old enough to fight in the War and foolish enough he knew to be a goddang Marine or some other damn fool thing to get hisself killed for those Marines they were brave tough sonsofbitches but a lot of them were dead. Also Cotton had heard that the land he came from in Oklahoma had been put under water by a dam or a flood or a curse and that the very spot upon which the old homestead stood was under water and although it seemed fittin to drown out such a place as God had drowned out the baduns in the flood he wondered for his little ones. He thought of his little brother and he was sad that he had left him all alone like that and he wasn't sure why he ever did bygod.

"Are you ok mister?"

the man running the counter asked of him.

"Yes" Cotton replied "Do I seem unOK to ya"

"Just that you have been sittin here for quite awhile staring off into space."

"I gotta lot to be thinkin about."

"What's a man with a backpack on his back walking up the highway got to think about besides the sun on his head and wind at his back?"

"He's got the wind at his back to think about."

The man running the counter scratched his chin for he knew what Cotton meant by what he said when he said he's got the wind at his back to think about.

"Well I don't know where you come from mister but I do know that there is plenty of work in these parts at this time of year. The Forest Service needs labor and maybe even fightin fires and there's cabins and motels need labor and parks and shops all over. You can get you a job up near Glacier Park if you have the mind to."

"Well sir" Cotton said as he stood and paid for his coffee with some change "I do have a mind to" then he was on his way with thanks to the stranger and feeling like Montana really was the place for him.

Now when a man does as much walking as Cotton does over the course of his life he might become uninterested in his surroundings as they become nothing but like the walls of his own house which he goes through every day and he forgets what's even hangin on them walls. And so it was with Cotton I guess you could say that every now and again he had forgotten what was hangin on the walls of his house his house bein the whole outdoors of the West but it wasn't like that here in Montana for he felt overtook with all the beauty around him like he had never felt he'd see. All them rising mountains rising up to button up to the sky like great white breasts in a pretty blue blouse and the river singing like a beautiful girl and the cows and horses along the quiet stretches of meadow was really more'n Cotton could even stand to bear but he bore it for it was so beautiful. He couldn't remember the last time he'd seen beauty so beautiful besides that girl Nancy back in Seattle who had wondrous breasts and hips and danced at night for money and lay with Cotton during the day this being the reason that he stayed too long in Seattle in the first damn place and had busted that banker's nose with a plate for saying his steak was too well done. Maybe he busted that banker's nose with a plate not so much because that banker was ornery which he was but because he knew he was sinkin in deep with this sexy burlesque Nancy girl and that that was no good so he had lit out without even tellin her and he figured it'd break her pointy little heart but he just couldn't care. He had to do it and he knew he had to and he did it and that's just the way Cotton was once his mind was made up. But all that to say he'd never seen such beauty as was hanging on these Montana walls he didn't think but this beauty did not make him want to run like he ran from that Nancydancer it made him want to nestle up in these mountain breasts and settle in the breath of the sweet wind on his cheeks and the blonde haired sun shinin down on him and just lie there and sleep. So Cotton went off the road a piece and he lay in the blonde haired sun with his most prized engineer cap pulled low over his eyes and he sawed logs like Paul Bunyan workin on a redwood.

His siesta was but short for he was awoken with a queer sensation of being kissed all over by beautiful dancer girls that loved and took care of him and didn't love no others like him all of em all at once and he sat up and saw that an ornery cuss damn cow had come over and was lapping up on his face like a dog would lap up water on a hot day and Cotton had to laugh but he still cussed at that bygod cow and told it to get for licking his face like that and givin him dreams of dancers when it couldn't even get him a glass of bygod milk. He wiped his face with his most prized possession cap and grinned and said

"Hell even the cows are rollin out the welcome mat"

and he felt mighty full inside like after you eat a good supper even though he hadn't eaten a good supper and he was getting kind of famished truth be told and it was a helluva far pace to walk to get to the Glacier Park to The Land Where the World Began as Indian father had told him.

5.

Cotton managed to hitch a ride from an old farmer who drove powerful slow in his old truck so that Cotton wondered why he didn't jump out and run on up ahead but he was glad for the rest to his legs and lungs so he just stayed in the cab and rolled a cigarette and offered one to the farmer who declined so Cotton smoked by himself. He didn't mind that the farmer didn't speak for he didn't speak neither but felt at peace just smokin with his arm out the window watching the land roll by real slow because the old man was drivin so bygod slow. After a bit of this slow drivin they came out of farmlands and cattle pasture right smack dab at the tip of one greatest lakes that Cotton had ever laid eyes upon which Cotton later learned was the largest fresh lake out West being Flathead Lake but it used to be called Salish lake and both names named after Indian tribes but Cotton didn't see no Indians. The old farmer did point out that this right here south lake was some rez land so he took Cotton a little further so he could drop him off with white folk and Cotton didn't tell him the Indians were his friends for he knew that that old farmer would not understand it.

"This old lake here" the farmer said and he seemed to be glad to have something to discuss with the smoking stranger with a busted nose as he took him into white county "is near to 200 miles all the way around when it's said and done."

"I'll be hornswoggled" Cotton said "That's a mighty big lake - good fishin?"

"The best. You gotta get licenses for everything nowadays but it's worth the trouble if you like bull and cutthroat trout"

and Cotton admitted that he did indeed love both of them trout though he could never be sure he'd et one or the other just trout in general and in his head but not aloud he thought that a license was never worth the trouble it was just something for the law to hold over your head when they needed to. Cotton had a car license once down in California god knows how but he did he took the test and all and later that month he'd lost it by drinkin and drivin and crashin when he crashed clean through a bar but that never stopped him from driving after that though it did stop him from owning a car himself.

"The Indians own a fair piece of the lake down here" the old farmer went on "and it's named after them. Used to be Salish Lake now it's Flathead Lake."

"Aint the Salish from out West"

"They sure are son you know your geography"

and Cotton felt a swelling of pride in his chest for another man especially an elder one at that although he be merely a farmer to tell him he knew something.

"They came out here I guess maybe because of the treaty and the land" the farmer went on "It's a fair reservation although there is some problems of course."

"Problems?"

"Poverty and drinking like normal" the old farmer went on and Cotton smiled to himself that he was just the same with his poverty and drinkin like normal and he wasn't even a goddamn Indian. "They shifted all those Indians around and now you can't tell most tribes from another."

Cotton didn't say aloud just thought that he had been shifted all around and couldn't tell his tribe from any other just like God's own people in the Old Testament but he didn't own a scrap of land so maybe the injuns were a mite better off than him although being chained to the land was what they were against in the first place and so was he so maybe just like he thought before the Indians really were his friends.

The old farmer dropped Cotton off and Cotton watched him drive back the way they'd came then he trekked up the road that looked down on that bygod beautiful Salish Flathead lake. Cotton hadn't seen anything so beautiful blue since he'd seen that blue eyed girl waitress down in Arizone who was going to college and workin. Man she was a damn hard worker as most women usually were he'd found especially since after the war even that Nancydancer in Seattle pulling all night shifts busting it like a mule. Looking at all that beautiful blue still lake deeper than God's eye sockets he had a great sudden sadness fill him at the thought of the lake and God and beautiful women so much so that he stumbled on a rock and to make himself feel better he cursed and threw that damned rock as hard as he could but it did not make it all the way down to the lake and his arm was sorer for having thrown it so hard for no damn reason so he cursed some more.

Every now and again as he made his way along the road he could pick out houses built into the trees some old houses and some newer fancy types which he didn't care for the look of. He almost wished that he could go back and live on Indian land but he knew that wasn't where The Land Where the World Began was it it was just a sad settling place so he went on.

Cotton made it to a fruit stand right off the road that was built like a red and white barn and it overlooked a small orchard that overlooked Flathead Lake with a man and his wife runnin the place so he stopped a bit and asked for some water for his canteen and they obliged mighty nicely and he got to talkin with them and soon he was helping them with some crates of fruit for which they gave him a nice dinner of venison and buttered taters all at a picnic table overlooking the orchard that overlooked the lake and he sat and talked to the man and the man asked him if he had been in the War and Cotton said that he had and the man shook his hand because he had been in the War as well and come to find out they had both been in the Pacific at the same time one doing building with the Seabees and one doing fightin with the Marines and I won't tell you which is which cause Cotton don't like to talk about it none. The husband and wife let Cotton spend the night in the fruit shed and told him to take all the fruit he wanted so he took a mess of tamaetas and peaches and apricots not so many as to come off ungrateful or beggarly then he lit out the next mornin before the man and his wife was up and he left them a note that said

"Thankee for your kineness - Cotton K."

and the man put the note in the money box like it was legal tender and his wife patted him on the back.

Cotton didn't know where he was going and he didn't quite care though he did a bit in the back of his skull but he couldn't tell why like a lightbulb with a dangling chain you can't find in the dark but maybe this is because hobos don't usually wander this far from civilization and the main tracks and Cotton knew it. All the same he just felt like something was pulling him along like the time he'd been in Wyoming wrasslin cattle and he had this lariat and he tied it around the bull's neck but the bull broke loose and Cotton's foot got stuck in the rope and he got drug across the damn yard with the other men laughing and he cussing and hollerin to raise up the dead and when he broke free he punched the bull in the head and they say it knocked the poor beast clean out then he went around and beat up the men that laughed at him and the boss fired him but gave him a couple week's wages for a good show. That's how he felt he was being drug so far from his beaten path was like by that bull and every now and again he'd look up to see if someone was laughin at him but they wasn't and it was ok and he didn't have to be so damn mad. So he drug on through a few small towns until he met the end of Flathead lake which is the Northern end and he was so sad to part with it that he made camp at the end of the lake near the beginning of a small town and he camped under the biggest sky he had camped under in all of his dang life. The only thing that made the parting with the lake and all its beautiful blue spirits bearable was the biggest bygod mountains on either side of him rising up like angel's alamos to keep out evil spirits which Cotton later learned was the Swan Mountains. The Swan Mountains went up like a mighty fortress that is our God and Cotton was betwixt them and he felt safe and like it really was The Land Where the World Began for God must of spent a awful lot of time here makin it and this made him think of God and he prayed even though he took the Lord's name in vain about a hundred times a day he prayed cause he felt like he was in Church and the stain glass nature windows hanging on these walls were spilling out their beautiful light on him and when he prayed he knew he wasn't as tough as he used to be and that scared him which made him mad because Cotton didn't get scared but then he figured even a man as tough as he could get a little fear in him when it came to the man upstairs. He reckoned gettin a little fear of the Lord in him would be ok out here all alone in the wilderness with no wild women nor men tryin to prove he wasn't something on a stick when right now he was not. He didn't even know what he was prayin for just checking in he guessed because he couldn't remember the last time he'd checked in. He didn't get on his knees and fold his hands as much as he sat on his ass and smoked a cigarette and inhaled the smoke like it was the Holy Spirit and he just thought them tobacco thoughts to God and he knew that this is how the Indians would do it and now he knew why they really smoked them peace pipes it was for to talk to God.

Then Cotton set out straight toward the mountain's pulp and there could be no mistaking that he knew where he was going now he was going into the heart of them mountains in the meaty part of this place like a hunter's bullet goes into a deer or like a man is drug behind an angry bull to the place where he must knock that angry bull out with his fists while the others stand around laughin.

6.

Now this is the part of the story when we are settin around the fire just watchin Cotton in our minds and we're wondering what could go right and what could go wrong for such a man as he. Least that's what I was wondering and I did not have long for to wonder for the very next day Cotton caught a ride clean into Stumptown which is the last town before you hit the government wilds of Glacier National Park being a town nestled up next to the mountains like a baby fawn to its doe momma. The mountains were still capped with snow a few of em and this town had a great lake near it not so great as Flathead but still deep and blue and ancient and pretty like that blue eyed waitress in Arizone but the best part about Stumptown to Cotton was that it had a mighty good looking train station for its little town size as it was a spot to catch The Great Northern or the Big G as Cotton had come to call it on account of ridin the rails so much and that's just what all the old hobos called it when he was a kid. So there was a great station and a railyard where they had some mining cars and lumber cars and all sorts of cars and it warmed Cotton's heart to see their many colors like Joseph's coat that his daddy give him. Cotton wandered the main street and was damned to find that it ended at the railroad tracks and on the other end of these tracks the town ended at a presbeterius church that was a square brick building with mighty fine stained glass windows and pine trees in the yard and a bench for to sit on. So there was a train on one end and a church on the other and all manner of shops in between just like the great Main Street of Life. If you sat on that bench in the churchyard and Cotton did then you could look down the whole of Main Street and see where the town ended at the railroad tracks and Cotton thought he'd never been happier in his life to just sit in the church yard and stare at the whole of the town and see the iron on the other end. He figured this must be what heaven was like being that he had been in hell quite a few times and knew the difference from his left and right as far as that was concerned. He was just sittin happy as a jaybird on that bench when he felt someone touch his shoulder from behind and he reared up and turned right quick with his fightin fists gnarl cocked and he said

"Here!"

which he says in a gruff mean hoarse voice and what he means by here when he says that is stop or what the hell or whatever else he means it to mean and I do not know where that comes from but Cotton has always said it and he said it now. He had his dukes cocked but he saw nothin but an old man in a black

46

get up and a white collar and he figured right away that this man must be the presbterius minister but he still didn't like him touching him like that for he was always looking for a piece of glass before him when someone came up behind him like that.

"Whaddya mean sneakin up on me like that!"

he hollers and the old minister seemed sort of taken abacklike and he says

"I'm sorry my son I just wanted to speak to you"

and Cotton replies

"Well next time you wanna speak to me you come round to the front door y' hear"

and the minister nodded his head and Cotton could see that he did hear and this is how Cotton met the minister and how he met the town.

"What brings you to Stumptown?"

the minister asked and Cotton said

"I don't rightly know maybe a bull or a bird I aint sure which but I aim to find out"

and the minister did not know what he meant but he could tell he meant it.

"Did you walk here?"

the minister asked and he pointed to Cotton's rucksack and Cotton didn't care for anyone pointing at his bag as you and I both know but he figured it was just a little old damn Holy Man so he said

47

"Not all the way."

"Are you looking for work?"

"I spose I am do you know of any"

"I do yes. The Forest Service has been looking for laborers. Summer work and hard but good work. Pays well and they put you up in bunks."

"That sounds mighty fine" Cotton says "Where might I inquire as to this labor"

"Well you can go to the park Headquarters up the road a bit but it might be best to do it first thing tomorrow. Do you have a place to stay?"

"Preacher do I look like I have a place to stay"

and the minister had to admit that Cotton did not look like a man that had a place to stay but went on

"You can stay here in the church yard if you like no one will bother you."

"Well that's mighty fine preach but I might feel kinda blasphemous buildin a fire on a church lawn"

and the minister says

"Why don't you let me take you to dinner? Then you wouldn't need a fire to cook your supper"

and Cotton being the shrewd grab as grab can man that is no beggar you see but shrewd just like any other business man who must eat says

"Why sure preach I could use a meal. Like my daddy

48

always said every time I move my elbow my mouth flies open"

and the minister being the shrewd grab as grab can soul saver that was trying to get to the real root of this wayward tumbleweed's sad lost soul says

"Oh is your daddy from here?"

and Cotton gets all quietlike and says

"G'day to you sir"

and was off with the minister standing lightning dumbstruck wondering after the wanderer and the minister knew he'd gone in too damn soon after the rabbit trap had fell on the rabbit and that damn rabbit had got away and there would be no supper tonight for stomachs nor souls so he stood and wondered what had just rolled into their Stumptown and what was going to happen and just like me and you he won't have to wait long to tell.

Cotton had but a few dollars left to his name by now though he looked like he had none. He figured he had two meals and six beers if he played his cards right but he knew he never played his bygod cards right so really he had bout three or four whiskeys and some odd change. So he hefted his bag and looked for a place to drink and he didn't have far to wander for there was all sorts of little places for one to wet his whistle. Cotton picked an old clapboard looked broke down place for he figured it looked the most least spendy as well as being close to the railroad tracks which was on the opposite end of the street from the minister who asked about his

49

daddy goddamn him and besides Cotton always felt at home near the rails so this is the place he went and it was called Dog Leg Pool Hall and it looked rough enough for him so he went in. It was dark and smoky and he felt it hug him like a long lost lady though he'd never been there before and Cotton was never foolish enough to get a hug from a long lost lady friend for once he was gone he was gone that's just the way he was. The long lost lady hug Dog Leg Pool Hall was filled with all manner of bygod roughnecks like John Henry railroad workers and Forest Service bucks with their green government workpants and bare white shirt sleeves and even some real lumberjacks just like Paul Bunyan only not quite so tall but looked just as rough. Cotton strode in like he owned the goddamned place and bygod he probably did cause when all the men seen him they knew he was a mean ornery cuss even though they didn't know him from Adam but some of them rail workers probably did by reputation if they had ridden the rails West to Seattle. Cotton ordered a whiskey though it should of been a burger for whiskey on an empty stomach is just a fight waitin to happen and you and I both know it bygod and so did Cotton but he was feeling like he couldn't care less on account of that old minister though he didn't mean no harm asking him about his daddy and that heavy feeling like an anvil was over his head of the earth arm barrin him and trying to force him to say uncle and he would not say uncle bygod he never had and he never would.

Just when about Cotton took a swig of his whiskey all of it in one swig a pretty girl comes out from the kitchen and she is waiting tables and takin orders and the men are all flirty with her and she's wearing a faded red dress faded by the big sky big sun and Cotton can tell that that dress has never been faded by any other sun other than the big sky sun and his heart kind of jumps up in his chest like when a deer hears a hunter and is off and running and you gotta go goddamn catch it. One of the most amazing things about this girl was her jet black crow hair she cut across her brow for some bangs that Cotton hadn't really seen like that except for a dirty magazine girl that he sorta fell in love with when he sees her in the magazine and this waitress girl had bright pretty blue eyes like she'd been born in Flathead Lake with all the Indians chanting her name brighter and bluer and more beautiful than that waitress down in Arizone and I don't think he ever thought of Arizona girl again. This girl is beer bottle pretty like his favorite beer with the girl in the moon hell this girl is even prettier he bets bygod and she is real life to boot. She's got a beauty mark if you must know above her lips those full lips on the right side and Cotton believes it is wild sexy so he digs in his sock and comes up with enough money for a meal that being the last of his money if he wanted more whiskey which he did and he ordered another round.

7.

So he waves this pretty pin up girl on over to him she just kind of smirking at his over eager beaver demeanor to see her for she is used to grown men older than her and roughnecks tryin to get into her drawers so she switchhips on over like she is the Queen of Sheba and says to him

"May I help you sir"

sort of teasing him like for you see he aint really a sir but a bum and he don't bat an eye he says

"No but I think I can help you"

and she says

"Now just how are you going help me?"

and he says

"I don't know but I'd sure like to find out"

and she shakes her head and sighs and says

"What'll it be mister?"

like she's damn sick and tired of all these beefy boys tryin to get into her drawers and Cotton being the man that he is he don't want to be just like all the other boys so he says

"I'll take a coupla yellow painted beagles hemorrhaging"

and she says

"What?"

cause she did not know what he meant by wanting two wieners with ketchup and mustard because he was talking like a damn hobo and short order cook in the big city. He sees the other men lookin at him by now knowing by his lingo he aint exactly straight so he lowers his voice and asks for a couple of hot dogs with ketchup and mustard and the girl goes and gets them for him and he likes to watch her walk for when she swings her hips it's like the scales and weights down at the General Store swingin and he can almost see a baby sitting on the right hip when it goes out wide that's how far wide she switched them hips.

As he is wolfing down his beagles a couple of locals belly up next to him and he knows they aint bellying up for just a drink so he just tries to ignore em but one a them says

"A whisky for the new guy"

and Cotton says

"No need mister I got my own cash"

and the man says

"I didn't say you didn't have cash just that I wanted to buy a stranger a drink is that a crime?"

and only then does Cotton turn to the man talkin and look upon him and by then he already knows he's no good but he turns to him just in case and there is no just in case he can tell he aint no good. This fella is a handsome younger fella with a modern slick lookin hair cut and a barrel chest and green government work pants and Cotton figures he might work with this man starting tomorrow so he don't want no trouble but he also don't want no goddamn drink bought with government money he aint earned his damn self. This nabob is grinning his nice white teeth at Cotton and that is the problem cause Cotton knows for damn sure that men do not grin at men they don't know just like a dog don't wag his tail at the mailman. Cotton notices the kid has got an anchor tattoo on the top of his right forearm but he knows this man is too young to of been in the War and Korea don't count bygod so Cotton says

"Leave off"

and he hears the room go all quiet and Cotton is bullheaded but not mushheaded so he knows the reason the room went quiet is because the rest of them in the Dog Leg thinks it is a bad idea to tell this particular man to leave off. Cotton also sees the pretty beer bottle big sky girl peek her head around the corner from the kitchen looking at him like he is a fool to tell anchors aweigh to leave off and he aint no fool and he won't have a pretty girl think so so

he orders another whiskey and the man tending bar
acts like he does not want to get it for him and he's
in the middle of a quarrel he'd rather not be but the
kid with the tattoo says

"Get it for him Carl"

and Carl goes to get it like that damn kid is the boss
though Cotton knows he aint the damn boss and
when Carl brings the whisky the kid goes to put the
money for it on the counter and Cotton grabs his
wrist quick like he was swattin a fly. Now the kid's
smile fades and he says

"Get your hand off of me mister"

and Cotton says

"Get your money offa my drink"

and it wasn't his best threat but he wasn't in the
mood for threats just he didn't want some young
buck thinking he could buy him a drink with
government money he aint earned himself.

Now Cotton knew that there are strings runnin
through all men like strings on his daddy's guitar
some of them strings being light and sweet when
you plucked them and some being dark and deep
and he could tell from the pluckin on this man's
strings that his strings were dark and deep just like
the strings on his daddy's guitar and his daddy's
heart. Now I don't know if this is right or wrong but
it is just Cotton that when he sees that this man's
strings are dark and deep like his daddy's he just
wants to pluck them more so he says

"You can take your money and shove it up your ass"

and he expects a fight to break out right then but it don't and the man behind the counter says to the good lookin kid

"Goddang it Terry take it upstairs that's what you want isn't it?"

and Cotton has no idea what anyone is talking about by upstairs but the kid smiles and says

"Let's take this upstairs mister"

and Cotton still don't know what they're talking about and the pretty girl she's behind the bar she says

"There's a boxing ring upstairs and the men place bets. Terry hasn't been beat for awhile."

"Well let's go upstairs and change that then"

Cotton says and he lets go of the kid's wrist and throws back his drink. As they head upstairs he turns to the pretty girl and says

"What's your name sugar"

and she figures it's the least she can do to give a dyin man her name so she says

"Jael"

and he says

"Like that babe in the Bible that John Henrys her lover's noggin" and by this he means the woman in the Bible that drove railroad spikes through her lover's brain like John Henry the spike drivin hero drivin against the steam powered drill and she nods amused that he knows this Bible bit about her name bein that he don't look religious one bit and in truth he aint.

"How much cash you got on ya Jael honey"

he asks her and

"Why?"

she replies all suspiciouslike.

"Just take the cash you got and put it all on me"

then he heads upstairs and Jael watches him go feelin kind of funny how he said put it all on me like he knew something she did not and so she did it bygod she gives all the cash she had in tips which was quite a bit being as how it was the busy shift after the men got off of work to the cook who is headed upstairs and says

"Put it on the drifter"

and the cook shakes his head at her like she has gone goddam crazy but he does it.

8.

Up above the pool hall restaurant bar that is the Dog Leg there is a whole damn boxing ring with ropes and all that looks like it's been there since Stumptown became a stumptown. Cotton can't believe he let himself be wrangled into this but he figures he needs the money so he says to a man takin bets

"What do I make if I win?"

and the man says

"A fifty"

and Cotton aint seen fifty bones in awhile so that sounds mighty fine to him though he don't know where they would get a fifty for no man is going to bet on him all against him but then he realizes they have a real professional gambling thing going on here and he can't tell if that is good or bad.

"And if I lose?"

"You get nothin"

the man replies and Cotton says

"Fair nough"

and he climbs on into the ring.

That damn Terry kid is in the ring bouncing around barechested like a jackrabbit and he looks like an advertisement in a magazine for a strong man or a weightlifter or some other such sissy thing. Cotton proceeds to take his shirt off and all the men stop and even Terry does for a moment in awe and I will tell you why. Lots of men have their stories written down in books and lots of men have them written down in papers and ledgers and wills and such but Cotton has his stories written upon his flesh since the time he was but a boy. He's got shiv lines and fag burns and knife slash scars and fire burns and a animal claw mark and bygod even a couple of bullet holes it looks like the men in the Dog Leg realize and get a bit worried about provoking such a drifter with such tales written upon his hide. He's got scars on his arms and chest and back and neck and even some strange blue tattoos that are faded like ancient bruises and the worst part is that these stories in skin are written over the meanest looking form of a body the men had ever seen like this goddamn drifter had been carved right out of the Rocky Mountains like some goddanged Indian legend. The girl called Jael winced when he took off his shirt she there standing in the doorway hiding to see what would happen to her cash that she put all on the drifter since he told her to and she winced for she had never seen a man with such tales told upon his flesh.

60

Cotton throws his shirt to the side on purpose covering the man who is taking bet's head and puts his dukes up and everyone looks at him like he is bygod crazy for they are about to give him some boxing gloves.

"Gloves" Cotton says "How're ya sposed to feel it goddamnit"

and the men feel kind of funny not in a good way deep down in their loins when he says this because that is one of the wildest things they have ever heard and they are some tough men bygod and even they aint heard the kind of language Cotton Kingfisher can dish out.

A couple of men help Cotton into his gloves and he is standin there in big sky Montana nestled between the mountains like a babe between a momma's breasts in a tiny Stumptown with the rails on one end and a presbeterius chuch on the other on the main street in a pool hall upstairs in some goddamned boxing ring standing barechested with his stories uncovered for all to see and he thinks nothing but scrapping thoughts. He thinks he will take it easy on this Terry kid because he may have to go work with him tomorrow bygod and he don't want him dead. And he thinks though he would kill me if he heard me say this and maybe I shouldn't but I know I will is that he needs to take care of his nose on account of the goddamn fruit pickers bustin it not long ago and kind of suddenlike he feels a bit unsettled that the earth is out to get him and this feeling is like a crow flappin in his ribcage. He stands there barechested the other side of this

Terry kid with his stories written all over him for all to see and he for some reason feels that crow in his ribcage flappin and he feels all small in the eyes of God and Montana and he thinks of his little brother and baby sisters and his momma's dog sad eyes and his daddy's broke guitar wailing and a bell rings like a damn train and he thinks he is on a train but he aint he is standing there in the big sky Montana nestled between the mountains like a babe between a momma's breasts in a tiny stumptown with the rails on one end and a presbeterius chuch on the other on the main street in a pool hall upstairs in some goddamned boxing ring and holy hell the fight has started.

He was drifting off in his tender thoughts of the earth having it out for him thoughts when Terry comes up and gets him right square in the face and it hurts bad enough with his broke nose to wake him the hell up but not before the Terry kid is letting loose a windmill hail of blows like a weathervane spinnin in the wind. As the blows rage upon Cotton he covers his head like he knows to do for he has not lost a fight since he can't remember when and this being part of it is to protect your head he learned early on by hard knocks to his gourd. He hears the men shouting as he is gettin pounded this Terry kid being one strong sonofabitch and he can feel those blows through the gloves like he wondered how he was supposed to feel em well he feels em now. He cannot seem to get a blow out cause Terry is taller than him and he is up against the ropes not believing there is a real boxing ring in this little place and he tries to think of the blows as being from his daddy

on account of that always gets his dander up in a
fight but all he can think about is his daddy's broke
guitar wailing. He hears the men jeer and holler and
hoot and now they are laughing because he wasn't
even a fight at all for Terry the bygod kid champ
and he feels sort of sad at all the men's jeering like
he's always tryin to shut men up and as soon as he
doesn't he feels he has let himself down and that's
just the way he is and I feel sort of sad even as I say
this about Cotton.

Cotton is getting pounded and the men are shouting
and he's trying to move about but Terry just keeps
on getting jabs in and Cotton thinks of his little
brother who he thinks is probably tougher than he
and maybe he was in the Service maybe they even
passed each other in the War could that be so he
wonders. He thinks of his sisters and how they was
babies and how in God's name did he leave them
there with that terrible man he does not know and
he don't want to think about it none yet he does as
he is gettin his ass handed to him on a silver platter.
His mind is runnin faster than his fists to be sure
and he is ashamed but he keeps thinking about his
family and he thinks about his momma and how he
heard she passed away I won't tell you how he heard
just that he did for some things about a man should
be left to the man himself to tell or not to tell. Then
he thinks as he is getting slugged but not yet going
down that he heard his momma passed and that
she was buried in the hills of the homestead but
he had also heard that the homestead was buried
under water by dam or flood or curse and he right
there in that boxing ring getting his hide tanned

realizes that his momma is dead and buried and not only that she is under water and he never put two and two together as far as that was concerned and even if he wanted to go back to say his peace to her grave he never could unless he swam to the bottom of some goddamned lake like a loon goin down for its supper and he wasn't a strong swimmer no more though he had been a lifeguard in California before the War and suddenly something inside him snaps like a dry twig under a boot in the forest and he feels a fire runnin up from his toes into his head like a whiskey fire only backwards cause it came up from his feet and as he is getting pummeled he snaps right quick to the side and hollers real loud and to this day not one of the men knew what he said although some say it was an awful filthy word. He roars and comes up outta his ass kicked position like a grizzly bear rarin up and he roars much like a lion he had heard in the circus when he did work for them back in his early drifting days and he goes one hundred proof crazy like he has in every fight before this one and every fight since. He steps to the side like a goddanged br'er rabbit jackrabbit and comes haymaking hard uppercut jump and busts Terry back like a man stepping on a landmine and Terry goes assbackwards stumbling back across the ring like as if he was drunk from that haymaker uppercut Cotton just thrown up under his jaw. Cotton goes mule buck ox ass crazy and Terry is caught on his heels and he's just a kid dammit and he aint ever seen such a man with such demons God bless him he's just a kid even if a snot nosed shit of one he's just a kid and he aint ready for the stories written on this man's body or ready to hear em told across

his own body. Terry stumbles back and Cotton goes
after him pounding away like he is poundin sacks
of flour or sides of meat he hammers and hammers
and Terry swings feeblelike and he hits Cotton good
a couple of times but there aint nothin for it cause
Cotton is possessed with what no one was sure but
they all knew he was possessed with it like he meant
it and the fire in his belly is boiling over and taking
Terry with it bygod. He aint just hitting and pulling
back like a graceful fighter no bygod he is hittin and
shovin his whole body from toes to fist up through
Terry's body with a roar so that the poor kid is like
to break in half if he don't give ground and slide
back into the ropes and then he is on the ropes and
Cotton starts beatin the everloving daylights out of
him on the ropes and what Cotton don't know is that
the jeering and hollering has stopped and it is silent
all but for his wild hollerings and his blows on the
boy's body that resemble a sledgehammer falling on
flesh which most men aint heard but Cotton has and
Terry's breaths being pummeled outta him and that
girl with the big sky big sun faded red dress has her
pretty beauty mark mouth open like she is catchin
flies and she has dropped her bar towel to the sweat
stained floor and she aint even thinking about the
cash she will win from this outcome. Then a bell is
ringing and Cotton thinks it is a train but it aint they
are trying to stop the fight on account of Cotton has
slugged Terry out of the ring and Cotton has come
out after him and proceeded to beat the hell outta
him outside the ring and all the men who are tough
men bygod have never seen such a thing and they
are scared as hell to pull Cotton off their champ for
they are afraid of the stories he will unleash upon

65

them so they pause then their better selves prevail for if they do not pull Cotton off they know he will kill Terry so a mighty rush of men all of them at once charge the Spartan and jump him.

9.

There are some years during Cotton's wandering that are missing like pieces in a puzzle and I guess that is for the best for a man has a right to tell or not to tell where he has or has not been though the puzzle when it is all said and done might seem incomplete. Some years like the War years are the toughest to figure and I know this is what Cotton would want so that is alright by me though I did wish I know what accounted for those years whether it be good or bad. I have heard some tall tales about Cotton living with Indians in New Mexico and his Dancin Dakota days and all and about some stints in prison but I cannot be sure and I guess I won't be tellin what I cannot be sure about. I do know of one stint in prison in Colorado when Cotton considered he had drifted too long like a piece of scrap on a river and it took him too close to the accusing finger of Oklahoma if you will look at a map and see what I mean and he wished he never had drifted that close to his old home and that time he drifted too far he was put in prison some men say for thievery but I know that is a goddamn lie cause he was no thief as

I was telling you before but I think it was more on account of his violent temperament just like in this boxing match we are watching because we all know Cotton is a damn ornery mule strong cuss who does not mind a good fight whether it be right or wrong. In that stay in prison in Colorado he managed to kick up such a fit like a cockfightin rooster in the prison yard that he started a goddang riot bygod with all the men fighting him then turning on one another til the guards had to shoot their rifles into the air but no one'd stop cause if they stopped they were getting sacked cause they sure as hell knew Cotton was not quittin being as how they had been in prison with him a few weeks and his reputation had been proved. The cockfight turned riot was so bad that they sent Cotton out of that prison that very same day because he was such a pain in the neck n ass and the Warden drove him to the State Line and uncuffed him and said

"And don't come back"

and Cotton replied

"I guess I don't reckon I will"

and the Warden turned the car around and left him standing there on the side of the highway on the Utah state line bygod and it was the best deal either man has ever made.

You might be wondering what that story has to do with the price of eggs in China and just hold your horses I am about to tell you for cryin out loud. I was going to tell you that Cotton made another best deal he has ever made the day he agreed to fight that Terry kid and to beat him and for that pretty red dressed Jael raven hair beer bottle beauty mark to put all her money on him and she did. It was a helluva deal and you will soon find out why and why I told you that other story to tell you he made another best deal of his life.

The men rushed him and jumped him and a bunch of em got clipped good and someone had to break a chair over his head not once not twice but three times to knock him out cold and as he lay there on the ground out cold where they had drug him off his victim Terry that Jael girl came over and stood looking down upon him layin there like a fallen angel that had fallen too far and hit too hard and she tried to read his scars but it was hard because they were hard to bear and women do not have a strong stomach for this sort of storytelling though it stirs something within em like the deep dark strings of man twanging within them. I reckon that this is on account of women having a piece of man in em coming from the rib of Adam when God made them that when they see a man such as Cotton and all his scars that the man's strings twang within them like the guitar strings inside the curvy body of a guitar echoing. I aint sayin I know this just that I suppose it and I guess no one can really dicker about it since I just supposed it. So this girl is there looking down on this drifter layin spread eagle on his back with blood spilling on the floor and bruises starting to form new stories on his flesh and the man that had taken the bets came over to the girl and said all angrylike to her

69

"Here"

not like Cotton says here to say stop or what the hell but to say here that he had a fat wad of cash to give her being that she had put all her money on Cotton just as he had said to do and she had won all the dough in the kitty bygod. It was a lot of money for all the men had bet against Cotton and if they had of won the bet they wouldn't have won but Jael's cash split amongst them as she was the only one that bet against Terry. Poor Terry was beat to hell and bleeding bad so they drug him out to the doctor but no one drug Cotton out they just let him lie there on his back bleedin with a greasy fifty dollar bill on his naked chest like a medal for winning the fight.

Cotton was dreaming of dancin girls and he was getting kissed but then something went wrong and he was in the water and he felt like he was drowning and he could hear dings and zingers and he was wading ashore into a blowing up hell then he sat up and realized they had thrown a bucket of water in his face and he was coughing and gasping and then finally laughing and

"Whooooeeeee"

he called out though he sees and hears wrens and robins and barn swallows about his head circling round and round tweeting like sonsofbitches and all the men stayed away from him for they had never seen such a thing as they had just seen especially for the man that had showed them the things they never seen to sit up and laugh and say whooooeeeee.

70

Cotton looked about and saw the place was a mess of blood and for a second he panicked like he had panicked before in his life but he does not want to talk about why he panicked before in his life and I do not blame him it's his story to tell or not to tell but he panicked now like he had before cause he thought he had killed Terry who was but a kid and he was supposed to work with him tomorrow. He looked and saw the Jael girl was looking at him and she was the only one standing with him and she saw him panic for a second when he thought he had killed Terry and she shared this moment with him like no other woman had for he had never panicked in front of a woman before and it was like a guitar string was plucked between them in the curvy body of the girl when she saw him panic then the panic passed and the girl says

"You weren't kidding about putting my money on you"

and Cotton says

"Do I look like a kidder?"

and she said

"No sir you do not"

but not sir like before when she had called him sir to mock him for bein a bum but now because he deserved to be called sir after that show bygod. Then this big sun faded red dress girl does something real sweetlike she sits down on her heels like a baseball catcher crouching at home plate next to this brawler and covers her knees with that red faded dress so as not to be improper and she hands him a wad of cash and he says

"Whatsat for?"

and she says

"You won it"

and Cotton felt all choked up a little he wasn't even sure why just that she had give him the money he guessed and no one had ever done something so nice for him though they had but when it's a pretty girl it's a whole helluva lot different it just is and we all know it and I mean no disrespect to Indian father or the husband and wife in the fruit stand nor any of the others who have done Cotton a kindness and neither does he mean them disrespect.

"I can't take your money"

he says trying to stand.

"Then why did you tell me to bet on you?"

"I meant for you to keep it I can get a damn job."

"Well I gotta damn job so take it."

"I don't want it I won my prize money"

he says and he holds up his fifty and she says

"Stop being ornery"

and throws the money at him and it hits his naked bloody chest and falls to the floor then she turns and goes downstairs and he is left alone outside the ring with the cash lying in bloody water at his feet. So Cotton picked up the cash and he went to the washroom downstairs and washed up and put his shirt back on and greased his hair and not to be outdone he goes and sits at the bar and orders beer and a steak though Jael says

"You should go on now"

but he refuses to go on now so she has the cook make him the fattest steak they have on hand and she serves him two beers at once and just keeps bringing em. The rest of the room is silent for most of the men have gone home and Cotton eats in silence just watching Jael's switchhippin but not saying anything just eating. When he finishes his steak and taters the best meal he has eaten since the fruit stand he pays Jael with the fifty then pockets the change she give him and when she comes out to see if he needs another beer she finds him gone and the wad of cash she threw at him sitting there on the counter as her tip and she smiles and feels sort of all choked up a little and she wasn't even sure why just that he had give her the money back that he had told her to put on him she guessed and no one had ever done something so nice for her though they probably had but it's a whole helluva lot different when it is an ornery mean cuss who is ox bow strong and mule kick tough that didn't care if he won or lost as long as he was fightin and you and I both know it. So she smiles and tries to hide it and she feels lonely all of the sudden like Montana is a very big place to be so all alone in.

10.

Cotton left the Dog Leg Pool Hall and found a liquor store and bought a bottle of whiskey and still had some cash to spare from his prize winning fifty. He felt stiff and sore and a bit hazy but good all the same for he had taught the earth what's what and he had a beer bottle beauty mark big sky pretty girl to dream about and he had whiskey to help him dream and to dull the pain of the fight. He went to the churchyard and sat on the bench and he drank the whiskey straight from the bottle and he heard the train coming into Stumptown whistlin Dixie and he closed his eyes and leaned back and thought wasn't life wonderful until he saw flashing lights on the back of his eyelids like he had seen before and he didn't care for so he opened his eyes and there was a small town police car and a small town police officer a cop Cotton would call him with his hand on his gun staring him down.

"Can I help you occifer?"

Cotton asks with a smile and the officer says

"You need to come with me"

and Cotton says

"Why this is a free country aint it"

"But you aren't free to beat a man half to death" the officer replies and Cotton thinks he has killed a man for a second not hearing the half part of the whole death thing the officer just said "so get in the car."

"I won that match fair and square just ask the kid"

Cotton says and the cop says

"I can't ask the kid you messed him up too bad."

"He aint dead is he"

"No. But he looks like he could be."

"He'll be alright in the mornin we had them damn sissy gloves on."

"Get in the car."

"Make me"

and the officer twitches like sweat is stinging in his right eye with his hand on his gun then Cotton laughs and says

"Just kiddin damn you then I will"

not even caring if he is getting arrested or not cause he has just whooped the earth's ass. The officer opened the back door of the paddy wagon and Cotton clambered in then they drove a block to the police station and Cotton laughed because it took longer to drive than it would of to just walk to the damn place. The officer took Cotton inside and opened up a cell and Cotton figured he at least would get a free bed for the night so he obliged until the officer said

"Hand over your rucksack"

and Cotton said

"Go to hell"

and he meant it and the officer could tell that he meant it not like when he joked make me so the officer let off a bit.

"Do you have a gun in there?"

the cop asked.

"No I've a knife but you can't have it"

The cop didn't seem like he cared much for the whole thing especially after hearing of the beating Terry had took so he let Cotton inside the cell with his bag even the whiskey in it and he locked the cell and Cotton drank whiskey until he passed out. The prison bed was the most comfortable bed he had slept on in a while hell it even had a pillow and he used his Indian blanket and was snug as a bug in a rug feeling warm from his head down to his toes and not just from the whiskey.

The next morning Cotton woke all groggylike and he stumbled to the front of the cell and pressed his face n arms through the bars and shouted

"Here! Here!"

but nobody came.

He cursed and was angry for he needed to go get a goddamn job at the Forest Service and he was hung over and buck sore and hungry but what could he do so he rolled a cigarette and started smoking it til about a few minutes later he heard the station door open and he looked up and at the front of the cell who should be bygod standin there but that fine Jael girl and he thought he was dreaming but he knew he wasn't.

"Is this a dream?"

he says even though he knew it wasn't and Jael says

"Do all your dreams end up in prison?"

and he liked her and thought she was clever so he smiled and said

"Nawwwwww just the good ones."

Jael was wearing a bright yellow summer dress with her black hair pulled back but for the bangs across her brow and Cotton saw that she had freckles across her nose and it made him happy to see like the stars up in the big sky or the wild Indian paintbrush flowers on the plains the other side of the Rockies. She pushed something through a slot in the bars and he said

"Whatsat?"

and she said

"Breakfast"

so he went and took the plate she pushed in at him covered in shiny foil and on it was a great mound of potato hash and scrambled eggs and bacon and he nearly wept for it smelled so good and she brought it to him and another one of this girl's kindnesses he wasn't sure he could bear to suffer like when she tried to give him back all the cash she had won on him fair and square. Then she handed him some silverware through the bars even though he had his own in his bag but she didn't know that because she's never seen the inside of his rucksack like we have thank God for she is a woman not a slob nor a hobo nor any kind of girl Cotton is used to in the first place and Cotton began to eat with Jael looking on though he knew his manners were terrible and he tried for them not to be but he was just a boy when he left home and his momma was never good with manners anyhow before he left so his manners were lacking and he knew it.

"I'd ask ya to pull up a chair but I've got none"

he joked and that Jael girl smiled kind of sadlike and he wondered why she would smile so sad when she was such a pretty girl in such a pretty dress in such a pretty place bein it The Land Where the World Began.

"Did I kill the kid?"

he asked as he bent his elbow and his mouth flew open.

"No" Jael replied "He was in the hospital last night

but they took him home this morning. He's got a lot of stitches and a broken nose and a few broken ribs."

Cotton squirmed a bit on the bunk where he was sittin when she said this because he knew he had no need to break any ribs in a boxing ring that even had a bell but he also knew that when he played he played for keeps and he could not care if someone cried over losing their favorite cat's eye. He wondered what the girl had come for but he didn't want to ask as to be too forward and he liked her company just the way it was so he said

"Thanks for the grub"

"I figured it was the least I could do for winning a bunch of money off of you. I've never gambled on the fighting before. I don't know what possessed me."

"I do it was me"

and that girl blushed though Cotton meant no harm over what he'd said and she knew it.

"Did y'bring this from the restaurant?"

he asked as he handed her back the empty plate through the bars.

"No I made it myself at home"

she says and this made Cotton feel warm all over like whiskey that she had cooked him a meal and had thought of him in her kitchen as he knew a kitchen was a woman's sacred place and to think of a man in it was a good thing for the man she thought of in it. He had been with women the last few years that did not see the kitchen as a sexy sacred place and it had always made him a bit put off by them. Jael stood there at the bars and he rolled and lit a cigarette and offered her one and she took it even though he had rolled it with his own hands and they were maybe a bit grubby she didn't seem to mind so he gave it to her and lit it through the bars and they stood smokin on either side of the cell.

"Thanks for the meal sister"

he says.

"You're welcome. Where you from?"

she asked blowing out smoke and damn she looked fine and sparkly through that smoke.

"Everywhere but here"

Cotton replies.

"Why are you here?"

"I heard that this is The Land Where the World Began and I figured I better come and see it and see if I could find me some Indians like back in the old days."

Just then the door jangled on open and an older police man came in that Cotton suspected was the younger officer who had arrested him's boss and this police man sees Jael standing at the cell with the bloody pugilist and he says

81

"What in the hell is going on here?"

and Cotton says

"That's what I'd like to know Capn"

and blows smoke through the jail bars.

11.

Jael left in a hurry like she wasn't supposed to be there and the police captain let Cotton out of his cage by saying

"They took Terry home from the hospital this morning and I can't keep you here as he isn't dead and that damn boxing ring is perfectly legal although if there was betting it isn't"

but Cotton didn't let on that there had been betting.

"If I had my way I'd take that damn thing down because it is just a place for trouble"

and Cotton can see this cop is all bowed up so he tries to unwind him by saying

"Aint that the gospel truth"

and the captain gives him a disapproving look like Cotton does not really think it is the gospel truth he's just saying that it is to please the captain and that dog don't hunt with the captain bygod so just cut it out.

"So maybe this aint the best time to ask where a fella can get a job"

Cotton goes on before the captain can get too angry at him for trying to fleece him over about the boxing ring.

"Son what in the hell are you thinking? You wander up here and beat the hell out of the town's main boy and then ask for a job? What is wrong with you? You're old enough to know better."

and Cotton suddenly gets hot under the collar for another man that is a bit older than him to talk down to him like that like he is just a snot nosed kid and he has to talk to the angel on his right shoulder to ignore the devil on his left or otherwise he is going to get into an illegal boxing match right here in the station with the captain being the next Terry kid he beats senseless bygod.

"I'm just a workin man that needs a job is all"

Cotton says and the captain goes to his desk and sits down all distractedlike and says

"Well that very well may be but why don't you first try not to beat the hell out of the townspeople?"

and as much as it galls Cotton as they say in the older testament of the Bible because gall is real bitter I think he says

"Yessir"

and this seems to work a bit on the captain.

"Are you getting out of town?"

"No."

The captain rubs his head all flusteredlike and says

"Do you have a place to stay?"

"No."

"Well you need to get a place to stay. You can't just be hanging out in the town causing trouble. Besides you never know when a few good old boys might want to jump you after what happened to Terry"

but Cotton does not think that anyone will jump him because all the good old boys had seen what he had done to Terry with their own two eyes.

"Now you go on down to the Hungry Horse Motel and tell them that Captain Carter said to-"

but when the captain looked up that crazy coot violent drifter was gone out the door with not even a word nor a sound and captain Carter was powerful angry for knew he was bound to have more trouble with that SOB and he wondered why in the hell he hadn't told him to skedaddle like a bygod stray but that's just the way it was with Cotton and when the captain ran outside it was like Cotton had disappeared for he was neither in the street nor the park nor anywhere.

Cotton hid in the back of a pickup truck outside the police station until captain Carter went back inside the station then he lit out to find the Ranger's Station that he suspected was up the road a piece so he started walking. Now as Cotton was walking he got to wonderin what a pretty sun dress wearing freckle faced crow haired girl would be doin bringing him a home cooked breakfast in jail and it made him feel goddamn good so goddamn good in fact that he felt he had a bird in a cage in his chest and the only way to let that lil birdie out was to sing so he did sing like he's heard his daddy sing back in the day you see Cotton did this every so often he would sing like his old man. Who knows what makes women do the things they do like put all their money on a man who is a sonofabitch and then win all the money they bet on him and then try and give it back to him then bring him breakfast in prison when he refuses to take the money back. Cotton did not know and neither do I but I guess this is what makes women so wonderous to men at least in part is their peculiarities that man cannot understand. All he knew is that he didn't think sad thoughts just good thoughts like about kickin the earth's ass all the way back to Kingdom Come and this made him laugh a little to himself but only just a little because kickin the earth's ass and laughin about it is a good way to make the earth angry enough to came rarin back at you and it is just rude besides that.

After a piece of walking up the road Cotton came upon a big outfit with lots of buildings and tourist attractions and campers roaming about but he didn't see no real Indians nor teepees though this was The Land Where the World Began to the injuns according to Indian father. Cotton went to the main building and he walks right on in and right on up to a lady at a desk who looks up at him and seems a little frightened on account of his appearance and she was for at first she thought he was a wayward hiker who had been mauled by a bygod bear.

"Came to find me some work"

Cotton said and the lady made him sit and wait and rings for a man to come to see Cotton about a job and also just to throw him out because he looks like he was just mauled by a bear and there is no reason for a man to look like he is mauled by a bear if he aint been and that is why she would like to throw him out.

Well a man with a Navy mustache came out and stopped when he sees Cotton and said

"Can I help you"

and Cotton stands up and goes to the man and shakes his hand and says

"So when do I start"

and the man looks at the woman at the desk as if to be cross with her for offering Cotton a job and she just shakes her head and presses her lips together to tell the man that she did indeed bygod not offer this here mauled bear man a job.

"What do you do?"

the man asked Cotton and Cotton replied

"A little bit of everthin"

and the man seems unimpressed by this and starts to tell Cotton why he cannot hire a man who does a little bit of everthin and Cotton sees him start to go into his windup to cut poor old maul bear man down so Cotton bein the shrewd business man that he is cuts the man off and says

"I guess if'n you don't need a veteran fire chief who is handy with a pulaski I'll be on my way"

and sure as the devil this man stops him from going for he knows that Cotton knows what a pulaski is which is a firefighting tool with a mattock and axe head put together named after the firefighter Big Ed Pulaski that made it so the man says

"Where were you fire chief?"

and Cotton replies

"Down in Oregon on the Coast have y'heard of the Tillamook burn?"

and the man had for there had been a few fires on the Coast there in Oregon that had burned the hell out of the mountains and they were big mean fires and sometimes on Oregon fire crews the Okies would bust it like a mule and Cotton had been one such Okie though he did not say this to the man but he could see the man had great respect for him when he told him about workin the Tillamook burn then the man said

"How would I know that is true about you working on the Tillamook burn?"

and as Cotton tells stories by his flesh and not on paper like by some bygod application or references or whatnot he pulls his shirt down a bit and on the right side of his neck down his back he has an ugly scar from a fire burn which was plain to see and he says

"Thisis how"

and the man has great respect for him just like the men in the Dog Leg when he beat the devil out of that sonofabitch Terry and the man is also intimidated by such a man as Cotton who would get such a burn and keep on tickin and the woman at the desk covers her mouth too see such a scar but what the woman at the desk does not understand but I do is that men don't always talk with words or with paper sometimes they talk to one another with scars and this is what Cotton and the Forest Service man were doin.

Well I will be tarred and feathered and so was the woman at the desk that after this exchange Cotton was hired right on the spot but that's just the way it rolls for Cotton and you and I know it though the woman at the desk don't well I guess she does now don't she.

So Cotton was hired on at the Forest Service before word of the hurt he lay on Terry the kid had chance to get up to the Forest Service Headquarters where Cotton stood and I will be damned bygod they even gave him several uniforms all green and brand new like the ones Terry wore and a place to stay since his work was seasonal and listen to this the best part was that they gave him a new truck for his own though he didn't even have a goddamn driving license.

12.

The tales of Cotton as long as the tracks across the States like train whistles in the wind tell about how Cotton was a hard ass worker on account of busting it like a mule and he had worked mighty hard on the Tillamook burn and they had asked him to stay on as a government employee but he had to get a move on so he did. Cotton did not wander because he could not or would not keep a job it was just that he felt himself being drug around and sometimes he would stay a day and sometimes a week and sometimes a month but in the end he would always get a move on and light out like an ember from a fire that leaves the fire and up jumps into the sky and then you can't see where it went that was Cotton. There were times that he had no reason to leave bygod he had every reason to stay like when he was young and in California and was a lifeguard and got to see all them beautiful girls in their wet delicates but that jackass stubborn Cotton went and left that paradise and when others that wandered the rails heard that about him leaving that paradise they wondered what had happened to make this man such a damn fool though they were wanderers in spirit as well and probably would of done the same thing as he. That was why it was worth taking note of the fact that he wandered off the rails and went into the heart of Montana like that and set to get himself a job bygod and he did.

Now it was Saturday and this must of been the reason nobody was missin that Terry kid and the Forest Service didn't need Cotton's labor until Monday but they set him up in a bunk cabin and no one else was there so he got himself all showered and shaved and cleaned up and tried to set his nose straight but he knew that was about as good as it was gonna get so he left it and combed his hair up nice and put on his crisp new green official uniform. One would think Cotton didn't cotton to uniforms no pun intended but he had worn them many times just to get by and he always wore them as if they were a costume like he has done in the circus back in the day and once he got his mind set on this mindset he was alright with wearin them as long as for not too long. Besides that work uniforms wasn't like suit and tie uniforms for he would never wear a suit and tie uniform and work in tall buildings bygod for Cotton figured if God would have wanted to make men wear suits he would have killed a suit instead of a lion to cover up daddy Adam and momma Eve but he didn't he made em wear animals skins and made em go out and bust it like a mule and this is what Cotton figures is right and he does.

So he went back into town lookin slicker n snot in his brand new duds just to show the locals what for bygod. He went right on back to the goddamn Dog Leg and the man Carl behind the counter who was the owner and had seen the whole thing yesterday says

"I think you need to leave mister"

after he gets over the shock that Cotton is wearing government green and is all cleaned up and Cotton says

"It's a free country aint it and sides I work for the Forest Service now so nuts to you"

and that Carl owner turned kind of greenlike like Cotton's uniform but he kept his mouth shut and gave Cotton a beer when he ordered it so nuts to him.

"Where's the girl?"

Cotton asked and the owner looks at Cotton like he's lost his damn mind and says

"Mister please let it be will you? We don't want any more trouble"

and Cotton is wonderin what trouble because he didn't start nothin in the first place bygod. He sits and smokes his hand rolled cigarettes and drinks beer at the bar and no one bothers him while he thinks good thoughts about the girl switchhipping even though she aint even there to see and he thinks about just a few days back from then to now which he usually don't because he does not like to think of time in a straight line like a fishing line in the water tight from a hooked gill but more like a snarled fishing line that you chuck cause it is wrecked but he does think straight now and he cannot fathom how much life has changed for the better in just a few short days and usually this makes him want to get a move on but now it don't so he sits in his smoke and he remembers about how the smoke helps him pray. So he's smokin and drinkin and poorman praying and he drinks a lot of beer though the man at the counter don't want to serve it to him none but is too scared to refuse and is confused as to how in the damnation Cotton got on at the Forest Service in the first place for godssakes. So Cotton is drinkin a lot of beer and he thinks about bein a boy at the homestead like he does sometimes when he gets an empty feeling in his belly like there is now and he gets mad at the hole in his stomach and he curses it but what can a man do. Once a preacher told Cotton that he was wrestling with God like Jacob wrestled the angel and this preacher said he walked with a limp in a spirituallike way like one who had wrestled an angel and Cotton said

"Preacher if I was wrasslin God I would hope he'd be big enough to beat me"

and the preacher says

"He is"

and Cotton laughs and says

"Well He aint beat me yet"

and winks at the preacher and the preacher did not like it one bit no sir so he prayed for Cotton after Cotton left and if Cotton knew this he would have been sore for a man praying at him like that but what he don't know don't hurt him hell in fact it helped him bygod as you will soon see.

So he is sittin there in Dog Leg thinking and he thinks that there was a family Bible in the homestead wherein he was raised and he wonders if it is underwater with his momma and he gets angry for his momma read the Bible and it didn't do her a damn bit of good nor her children. Cotton had never cared for the Bible when he was young for it told him to pray to God like God was a good daddy but Cotton did not know what a good daddy was so he just prayed to God like He was a distant relative and God still did not save him from his daddy or any other old thing so what was the goddamn good. Cotton begun to think that he did not want to be covered in blood the blood of the lamb or any other for that matter but what Cotton does not know is that he has been covered in his own blood and many others his whole life through his vile temperament and violence and each time was like a baptism of bad blood maybe I don't know and I don't want to be blaspheming God none God help me I am just sayin what Cotton is thinkin Good Lord if you are listening.

Cotton gets plumb wore out just sittin back on his thumb thinking Christ thoughts and momma thoughts and Bible thoughts so he gets up and pays his bill and gets the hell out of the Dog Leg and outside it is dark as hell but all the stars're shining like little Christmas lights that Cotton sees inside windows and on people's houses but he has never owned any himself and he cannot believe how grand all the stars in the big sky are like sparkling angel's teeth and Christmas lights. He is standing there dumbfounded lookin up at the stars when he hears someone call to him and he thinks he is dreaming about his momma but it aint his momma it is that girl Jael who brought him breakfast in jail and he thinks he is dreaming but he knows he aint but he says

"Am I dreamin"

though he knows he aint and this sly pretty girl says

"Do all your dreams have me in them?"

and Cotton says

"I wish bygod"

and she blushes a bit but there is no harm done cause no one can see her cheeks go red like a wildflower for it is big sky dark out there then Cotton says

"What in the hell are you doin here"

and Jaelgirl lookin all pretty even in the big dark says

"I live here Cotton or have you forgotten. I came to tell you the police are looking for you to give you hell and make you leave Carl just called them"

and Cotton knows that Carl is the Dog Leg bar owner and he knows he will give Carl a piece of his mind by his mind he means a knuckle sandwich with extra sauce the next time he sees him but right now that little girl grabs his arm and man I will be damned her grip is firm and leads him down the big sky dark sidewalk and into a joint which come to find out it is a bowling alley bygod well lit and lots of families and Cotton goes blind with the lights and it is loud and there are lots of children hollering and whatnot.

By the time he can get his wits about him he is in the bowling alley and he says

"I can take care of myself bygod"

seeing as how the girl is trying to hide him from the cops and he don't need no goddamn girl hiding him from no bygod cops and Jael smiles at him and says

"I bet you can bygod"

and she is teasing him by using his favorite word and he likes it so he rubs his face kinda self conscious like because his nose is fighting crooked and hell it always has been.

Jael pays money for them to have bowling shoes and a pitcher of beer though Cotton says no woman will buy him nothin well she does and tells him to go to hell besides and Cotton likes it so he lets her. So Jael sits down at a table next to their bowlin lane and Cotton is bamboozled like he don't know why the hell this girl is bein so nice to a goddamn drifter like he but not wanting to say such a thing to her for fear she won't be nice to him no more so he just fills a mug with beer and swallows it whole.

"You sure can drink" Jael says "but can you bowl?"

and Cotton says

"Honey I aint met a girl who can best me yet"

and Jael proceeds to best him yet and whoop his ass in the first game and more and he does not even give a damn which aint like him at all he usually gets powerful angry over losing hell even more so to a girl but for losing Cotton pays for all the beer and they are drinking mighty fine and the families are covering their younguns ears because Cotton is cussing like a goddamn merchant marine or maybe just a goddamn marine but cursing something fierce anyhow and Jael don't seem to give a good goddamn and she is laughing. Cotton is happy as a dead pig in the sunshine though he feels sillylike in these goddamn bowling clown shoes that looks familiar from his days in the circus with Jael winning for he gets to watch her from behind in her polka dot skirt as she bends to huck the ball down the glossy alley and the hole in him that he was talking at earlier at the bar is gone for now and there is just a jonesing for that big sky girl to come childbearing switchhipping on over here and sit on his lap and call him daddy and he will call her his sweet boogahoney hot damn.

13.

After a few rounds of bowling and beer the drifter and the pretty girl set at a table to smoke and drink more beer and Cotton says

"Why're you so goddamned kind to me I'm about to get suspicious"

and Jael just smiles and shrugs and says

"I think you're alright"

and Cotton says

"I'll take it"

and the girl goes on

"Those men were picking on you and they deserved what they got when you beat them. Carl told me to give the money back that we won but I said no so he fired me."

"Fired ya bygod?"

Cotton says and he is fiery furnace fit to be tied at

Carl the owner of the Dog Leg for Carl is a worthless no good sonofabitch welcher that fires girls for winning a bet fair and square off a man who won a fight fair and square.

"Don't get all riled up"

Jael says and she waves her red fingernails in the air like she is swattin a fly and Carl the Dog Leg owner is the fly and goes on

"I don't give a damn I can get another job. That place was a hell hole. That is one of the boys tricks. They find strangers who don't know any better and they lure them into fight then they beat them up and take their money."

"Well I guess I know why you bet on me then" Cotton says "They picked the wrong SOB to mess with I reckon"

"I reckon so"

smiles Jael and she is real pretty when she smiles like that under her black hair cut across her forehead and when she teases Cotton he reckons.

"Next time just try not to kill Terry and make the whole town mad is all"

"I guess he had it comin and I don't pull any punches bygod"

"No you certainly do not. Where'd you learn to fight like that?"

and just for a flash Cotton's a mind to tell her on

his early hobo bareknuckle brawl boxing days when he'd box for money in dark alleyways and seedy dockyards then Cotton can see this girl is starting to get him chewin the fat and he's been drinking and he will need to be careful about this one like Adam should of been careful with Eve so he says

"Hell I came outta the womb kickin"

and Jael thinks it's charming but she don't bite the bait and Cotton can see that though she appreciates his charm she does not bite and this is the first girl he thinks he's seen as such and he thinks it's charming and he bites.

Now while Jael and Cotton are sittin there bending each other's ears back I was going to tell you how I was wonderin why a man would sit at the fire and open up his palms to the fire when his palms is such a small part of him needin that fire but a man always puts his palms nearest to the fire first naturallike like God made him do it so I was at a fire and I opened my palms to it just like I said any man does and it sent a great God warmth into my palms that shot all up in my body like a swig of whiskey then I knew why men do that is the palms are like metal to a magnet for the heat. I say this to talk about how a man is like this to a woman the man bein the palms and the woman the fire and man just naturally sidles on up and takes all the warmth of the woman she gives him and it runs all through his body like a swig of whiskey this just being the way the good Lord made it and this is how it was with Cotton and that Jael girl she was warm and he was open palms gettin a dose of her fire that went all through his body like a swig of bygod whiskey this is why I told you that about the palms and the fire.

The pretty fire and them rough palms sit and talk and smoke and they do not say much about anything though they talk a whole helluva lot until the place shuts down then they stand on the sidewalk under the big sky stars and the Blackfeet wind is blowin and Jael's teeth are gleaming in the night and Cotton wants to give the girl a good hard kiss but for some reason he don't he don't even try and he wonders why he don't even try but he don't and that is all there is to it dammit. They say goodnight and Jael says she had a good time and she will see him around town and when he hears this he says

"Unless I see you first"

tryin to be all cute but he knows it is jackass beer talk and it just slipped out like a jackass braying and he is about to ramble on some more and that would have just been more mule braying but the girl is gone off down the sidewalk into the night with a laugh like a hoot owl in the dark.

Cotton manages to drive the National Park truck to the cabins he is staying at on a government dime without wrecking it all up though he drank a hellton of beer and he goes and falls dead into a bunk and passes out thinking sweet thoughts of big sky round hips and glacier firm rising breasts and juicy ruby reds under a dot of a beauty mark and as he drifts off to the big rock candy mountains he thinks that that little girl Jael told him a story about the cops comin after him she just told him that to get him to come with her bowling and that is mighty fine for him bygod.

Cotton gets up the next morning and finds Jael has slipped him a twenty dollar bill from her fight winnings into the pocket of his work shirt and it makes him angry as all hell but not as angry as the fact that someone is in the cabin john when he tries to go see a man about a horse so he goes outside and takes a leak on a great grandfather pine then realizes that there are people out there tourists bygod wanderin on past the worker's cabins rubberneckin at him so he lights a cigarette with his fly undone and hollers at em

"Enjoyin the show"

and he keeps on leaking and the people googly eyein him get a move on bygod.

When he goes back on in the bunkhouse there is a man at the stove making what smells mighty good and he does not turn when Cotton comes in so Cotton says

"You must be the new guy"

just jokinlike for see he is the new guy and the man turns around for Cotton to see he is a Indian kid and Cotton is happy to see this though this Indian kid he does not have long hair nor feathers nor native garb. Cotton is happy to see an injun roommate besides for he knows Indians are hell of firefighters for he has worked with them hot shot red hat crews from Navaho rezs and he knew some of them besides from the War.

"Are you the new man?"

the Indian asks and Cotton says

"Yep what's your name"

and the Indian says

"Jacob Two Calves"

and as much as Cotton respects the Indian last name he can't keep his mouth shut about the whitebread Old Testament first so he says

"Jacob what kinda Indian name is that?"

and the Indian turns back to the stove and is silent and Cotton feels a bit foolish about offending a goddamn Indian about a bygod name but he can fix it so he goes on

"When do we start?"

and Jacob the Indian says

"It is Sunday. We start tomorrow"

and Cotton says

"Alright then Jacob"

on purpose calling him by his Christian name so to speak to make peacepipe about that name that Cotton made fun of but the Indian don't say nothin so Cotton sits on his bunk and thinks about Jael and smokes and then the Indian hands him a plate of food for no goddamn reason he does not even know him and he made fun of his name to boot and Cotton is much obliged of course and they eat in silence and it is tasty beef steak though Cotton wishes it was bison but it aint and eggs and some sort of native mash or some such Indian meal Cotton wagers. Cotton is fond of it the mash and he tells Indian Jacob so and Jacob nods his thanks. Cotton is partial to all sorts of victuals being that he is a well traveled man and has a hollow leg as his daddy would say for he is fond of okra and beans and grits and sprouts and cabbage and tamaetas as well as venison and mackerel cakes and pork and beef and mulligan stew and succotash and wild duck rabbit and grouse and cornbread and biscuits of course and buckwheat pancakes with stewed peaches and candy bars and hamburgers and hotdogs and fried chicken and mashed taters and brown gravy on a slice of white bread or any type of shit on a shingle and hand rolled cigarettes as well as beer and sweet tea and black coffee and hotsauce as well as whiskey as well as champagne. The only time Cotton ever drank the blonde bubbly was when a pretty little thing who was blonde and bubbly brought it for him and he and this blond bubbly girl got paint the town red faced and had the time of their bygod lives before Cotton left her the very next morning as soon as the fog in the air and his head lifted for any girl that will bring you the blonde bubbly is playin for keeps and Cotton wasn't a keeper so he left.

I told y'all this just so you would have somethin to know about Cotton as he sits there in silence with his Indian so you do not wonder what was happening for nothing was and is. They are just sitting silent as they eat for Indians are silent people Cotton has come to find a lot of them anyway and he thinks it is best not to bother them and this is awful polite of Cotton as you might know.

14.

Cotton and Jacob Two Calves sit and smoke Cotton's hand rolled cigarettes which Jacob seems to like a heap after this hearty breakfast and Jacob Two Calves is a mighty fine person Cotton wagers for he tells Cotton after he warms to him a bit all about how he is Blackfeet Confederation but Blackfeet aint even the half of it for Blackfeet is a white name for a bunch of different tribes bygod and Jacob is actually a Blood Indian which Cotton likes very much for he likes the word Blood. Jacob says he is from the rez that borders the park and jumps clean on up into Kanada for white men have borders but the Indians don't have white man borders and Cotton likes the sound of all the Indians up here in the meaty part of Montana. Jacob goes on that he comes to work here at the park in the summer and he loves this place for it is beautiful and Cotton tells him about how he heard it is The Land Where the World Began from Indian Father down South then Jacob says it is so and tells him about Old Man and how he created the mountains and the lakes and the rivers and streams and animals and even the first man and woman and how he showed em about food and fire and even killing buffalo by running them off a cliff and Cotton is thinkin real heavy as Jacob Two Calves tells him all this just slumping on his bunk slow smoking and life feels just about right and he feels like the earth aint out to get him especially if Old Man made it.

"Where's Old Man now?"

Cotton asks for he figures he aint seen Old Man unless by the work of His hands in these here mountains and he wonders if Old Man is the same Lord God from the Bible and Jacob says

"He has gone away but he will come back and bring back the buffalo"

and Cotton says

"What happened to all the goddamn buffalo anyhow I'd like me a bison steak"

and Jacob Two Calves goes on about how the tribes of Indians were hit mighty hard by white men bringin smallpox and wipin the buffalo out and Cotton figures that he is speaking with a real Indian like he has been looking for his whole life when he came out West even though this kid does not have feathers in his hair nor Native garb. Cotton likes the look of his face for it is like a dark polished leather laid upon stone with warm brown eyes and Cotton thinks Jacob must be young and old all at the same time as he speaks real plain about the Indians losin their old ways. Cotton thinks it makes the hole inside him ache just a touch to think about all them damn

Indians losing their land and their happy hunting grounds and even their buffalo bygod and it aches a touch just like it aches when he thinks about how he lost his land and his hunting grounds under water with his momma and he don't even know where his tribe is. He thinks as he smokes that he wonders why men always have to try to tame the wild wanderer like he and the injuns and put fences up on him and he feels like he knows Jacob Two Calves better than he has known anyone else like they are brothers and he thinks this as their cigarette smoke rises up and drifts together til you can't tell whose smoke is whose and that mixed up cloud of smoke drifts out the open cabin door and into the Blackfeet wind and into the Glacier mountains Where the World Began and Cotton imagines Old Man can smell their smoke and is smiling down upon them from the sun and Cotton wonders when Old Man is comin on back to bring back the buffalo for he could use a bygod bison steak.

The next morning is Monday and Cotton does not even know it for he never knows what goddamn day it is that's just the way he is but it is Monday and it is time for work bygod and Jacob Two Calves who is sharing his cabin wakes him up and they drink some coffee then they all meet at the work shop headquarters and there is an army of men all dressed in government green. Cotton feels like just one of the boys which he aint sure is good or bad it just is so he just listens to the man talk and hand out jobs.

Now Cotton is lookin for Terry the kid and he spots

him bygod across the way standing with some of the crew that Cotton seen him with in the Dog Leg the day he beat the spit out of him and whoo boy does Terry look like shit on a stick he looks like he's been run through a ringer the ringer being Cotton with stitches and bruises and whatnot. Cotton figures he must be a tough bastard if he is working with broken ribs and he thinks maybe this kid is alright but he does not think it too long because he knows he aint he's a mean string like his daddy that won't stop hummin when you pluck him. When Terry sees Cotton across the way he nearly lays an egg and Cotton smiles at him and waves and this is how Cotton begins his first day at the Forest Service and the man that hired him besides gets up and says

"We have a new man aboard. I know it might seem a little unexpected but he is an experienced fire man and we are in fire season gentlemen. His name is Cotton Kingfisher he's bunking here with Jacob Two Calves that we all know from the last couple of years on fires. I want you to pay him heed if there is a fire and he will be the first man in if he is near it. I have given him use of one of the equipped fire trucks with all the tools and he has a radio in there as well so you give him and Jacob a call in case of fire. Cotton has fought the Oregon Coast fires and he is very experienced"

and Terry turns bright tomato red and Cotton thinks he sees smoke comin outta his ears and there probably was bygod for the man who beat him within an inch of his life has got a job right next to him and the other men look at Cotton too and he

110

looks tough as hell and they figure it to be about right for him to go into the fire first.

Then the crowd breaks and Cotton and Jacob are sent up an old road to go dig out a creek that got dammed by a falling tree and so they do and it is sunny and peaceful and Cotton feels Old Man smilin down on him in the warmth of the sun and every now and again he looks up and grins at Jacob and Jacob grins back and they bust it like a mule under the big sky Old Man big sun.

Cotton works so buck hard that Jacob tells him to take it easy but he won't bygod so they are done with twice as many tougher jobs than all the other men by the time the day is done and the Head Ranger with the Navy mustache that hires Cotton comes to their truck and says

"Cotton Kingfisher I have never had a man work so hard for me in all my life"

and he shakes Cotton's hand through the window and Cotton laughs on his way back to the cabin but what laughin the Old Man hears in the sky that kid Jacob don't in the truck because the poor kid is passed out sleeping for Cotton plumb wore his Indian ass out.

Cotton is fit to be tied at Jael for giving him a goddamn twenty dollar bill like he is some mooching hobo that cannot make his own twenties so he leaves Jacob at the cabin to nap it off and he goes right on down into town lookin for that goddamn girl. He parks his truck and walks down Main Street and just looks in every store looking for that girl but he does not see her so he is standing smokin by the church and a train is comin in and he feels a tingling deep down within him as the many colored cars like the coat of Joseph that his daddy give him slide by at the other end of town. He is thinkin and thinkin and he hears someone behind him and he turns real sharp like with his dukes up and hollers

"Here!"

and he will be goddamned if it aint that little old man of God minister at the presbeterius church sneaking up behind him again and he hollers

"Preacher I will hit you so hard on the head you'll be lookin out your ribs thinkin you was in jail! What in the hell is wrong with you sneakin up on me like that bygod"

and the preacher can't believe it is the same buck wild hobo as he met the very first day he was in town now wearing park ranger green but also he thinks it must be fate and he knows that fate is just a tiny word for God so he says

"Hello my son! I am so happy to see you"

and Cottons growls

"Oh I just bet you are"

and the preacher says

"So you found the job you came to seek"

and points at Cotton's uniform.

"Sho nuff" Cotton says cooling off a bit from that sneaky preach who should not sneak up on a man like that for obvious reasons "I started today and it was damn fine and I think I might finally be beatin the earth"

and the preacher thinks this is curious but he also sees it as a way to speak with Cotton on other more pressing spiritual matters so he says

"Do you think you need to beat the earth?"

and Cotton responds

"Well it's been beatin on me since I was a baby so I spose I do"

and the preacher says

"Maybe the earth just wants you to make peace with it"

and Cotton says

"The earth don't need you to make peace with it preacher the earth just wants you back"

then he is off down the street and the preacher watches after him and he wonders about this buck wild wise man who seems wrong in what he is wise about but maybe wise just the same.

15.

Cotton went off on down the sidewalk with the preacher thinkin preach thoughts after him and he did not need them no sir so he went to the market to get some goods for supper so that he could repay Jacob Two Calves for his breakfast he made him. He walks into market and who should he see bygod but that Jael girl and sweet Lord she is wearing denim jeans rolled up to show her ankles and her hair is in a pony tail and Cotton after he gets over how shiny she looks he marches over to her and whips out the twenty from his pocket and puts it in her face and says

"Did you do this?"

and she looks surprised like a flushed grouse out of the bush but then laughs and says

"You bet I did bygod"

and Cotton's leather face cracks a grin and he says

"You take it back bygod"

115

and she says

"No"

and he leans in and says real lowlike

"Missy I've a mind to tan your hide"

and she bats her eyes like a goddang cartoon and says

"First you should ask my dad"

and around the corner comes get this no lie the cottonpicking police chief captain sheriff guy that let Cotton out of his cell for he could not keep him because Terry had not died. Cotton cannot believe his bygod assbackward luck that the captain is Jael's daddy so he calls out

"I'll be hornswoggled"

and he would be damned to boot if it was up to the captain because the captain thinks this here drifter is a helluva cuss and a even more helluva problem and he stops in his tracks in his khaki uniform and shiny star and says

"What in the hell is going on here?"

and Jael says

"Daddy this is Cotton"

and the captain looks all off kilterlike like how the hell his daughter is on a first name basis with this criminal cuss even though he saw her bringin him breakfast in prison for who knows what reason bygod and he goes

"I know very well what this man's name is! Now Jael Dorcas Carter go get in the car"

and Jael says

"Dad I am twenty four for Godssake I am not a child"

and her daddy says

"Go. Get. In. The. Car."

just like that with stops and all I swear. There seems to be a real showdown at the OK corral cookin here I tell you for Jael is crossing her arms now which makes her big sky big Montana breasts sort of swell up like a wave on the sea good Lord amighty and she aint a girl she's a woman and her daddy is talking to her like she is a girl and Cotton can see what her daddy can't see by that swell on that lovely sea that she is indeed no girl but a woman and she is a delicious woman at that and a cuss.

"All I wanted to say is that this pretty little miss who seems to be your daughter has dropped a twenty dollar bill"

Cotton goes on to get the girl out of hot water with her daddy and he takes the twenty and hands it to the girl as she shakes her head and he says

"No no now that's yours sissy I saw you drop it. I was just doin my duty Capn"

and the captain looks at Cotton like a monkey's

uncle to think that Cotton would think that he would believe he was just giving his little girl daughter a wayward twenty but Cotton cuts him off and says

"Got a job Capn see my stripes"

and he points at the badges on his uniform that signify he is a government employee of the Park and Cotton can tell the captain's head is about to blow a top and just when about Cotton is gonna yell fire in the hole over the Capn's exploding head the captain calms himself and says

"I called Fred Mason up there and told him about you mister"

and Cotton knows Fred Mason is the very man who hired him the Head Ranger with the Navy mustache and he says

"I guess you were a tad late"

because he is already wearing government green and the captain couldn't stop him and when he says this Jael laughs a little and her daddy turns to her as if he is just astounded at her like his favorite family dog has suddenly come down with the rabies and then he goes on

"Well you better watch yourself mister because I talked to Fred just today and he's onto you"

and this bows Cotton up a bit but also tears him up for it feels like daddies are always out to get him and he is too old to be having daddies out to get him no more so he says

"Well now that I have replaced the lost money I will be getting back to the Park"

and he turns and leaves Jael and her daddy standing in the market aisle he without a scrap of food in his hand and them just standing there at odds like a couple of roosters at a cockfight.

Cotton drives on back to the cabin thinking of his terrible bad luck about how Jael is the captain of police in Stumptown's daughter and how he will never get to kiss those sassy ass beauty mark lips though she seems sort of fond of him though he never really knows why. He's angry at the captain for treating him like such and he is sick of men treating him like such like he is a criminal for he aint bygod sure he's gotta temper but who don't and hell Terry asked for it and when you ask for it you get it and no one should horn in when you get it what you asked for for it is what is comin to you. Cotton had the earth beating on him since he was but a baby and hell he never had anyone horn in for him but always look down on him and get all riled up at him so to hell with them. Then Cotton's mind wanders and he wonders why such an Old Man big sky daughter of the mountains like Jael would bat her eyes at him like she is a goddang cartoon.

Now as I told you before Cotton had no trouble with the ladies no sir but this Jael girl was different than the ladies our Cotton was used to she wasn't a nudie dancer or barfly or show you her breasts in the hall with a wink type of girl bygod she was like a silver dollar to a crow all shiny and pretty and a little rough but not city rough mountain rough and that

119

is a whole helluva lot different and we know it. But here is the thing about Cotton that he sells himself short on though he knows he's a charmer is that he is a damn handsome man. I do not mean to say that I know what exactly a handsome man is to a woman bygod but just that he is striking like lightning when you see his leathered stone face that has story lines written all in it and upon it and his crooked fighting nose that has always been that way cause he is always fighting. He has got a steam shovel iron jaw and eyes like coals beat into diamonds and he looks mighty like he is an old Bible king that has been run through the wringer that is America but the lines on his face and body just add more to his bearing and women I tell you they like this they like a man who has lived a life and it is written on his face a face that is handsome and bygod Cotton was both. I tell you this so you know in a way what Jael sees in Cotton that he don't it is that he is the most handsomest man she has ever seen even more than Terry the kid which I will talk about in a bit and the very reason Cotton doesn't know why she would cotton to him pun intended is the very reason she does is that he has lived more and it shows on his face and there is nothin much on Terry's face but the lines that Cotton gave him.

So Cotton goes home thinkin about Jael and he forgets he is hungry until he gets to the cabin and Jacob the Indian is cooking up some canned hash and eggs and toast and him and Cotton eat a hungry horse meal after their day busting it like Jacob hasn't ever when there is a knock on the door and it is Fred Mason come to talk to Cotton so Cotton goes outside with the boss man all prepared to turn in his uniform and forget about the girl and hop the rails in Stumptown.

"Captain Carter called me today"

Fred Mason says and Cotton says

"So I gather"

"And he says you beat the tar out of Terry Clay"

and Cotton says

"If that is his name"

and Fred says

"It is his name. I saw him today and I thought he'd been in a car accident he looked so bad and he told me he had been I suppose because he didn't want to admit you'd beat him so bad. Now I can't have violence on my crew you hear that right?"

and Cotton says

"Yep"

and starts to unbutton his green government shirt right in front of Mason and Mason says

"What are you doing"

and Cotton says

"I am leavin just like you're askin"

and Fred Mason said

"Who said anything about leaving?"

16.

Cotton had always known to get when the gettin was good and this had begun back with his daddy you could say. He had waited in that tree for his daddy to come out and skin him alive after he had broke his guitar over his head but his daddy didn't come and get him he just cried and cried until he blacked out so Cotton crawled down from the tree and went and peeked in the door and his daddy was layin on the bed cradling his busted guitar and his wife who was Cotton's momma was lying next to him and his momma seen him look in on them and when she sees Cotton she raises her hand at him and Cotton could not tell whether she was telling him to go or stay but it seemed her dog sad eyes were cryin either way and Cotton knew the gettin was good so he got and he never looked back. This is how he is to this day so when the Forest Service Boss Fred Mason came to talk to him that night about fighting and the captain calling he figured he'd get while the gettin was good but it was not as good as the staying for Mason said

"Look I can't have you getting violent around here I don't care what fire you fought on. But I know you are one hell of a worker and I know that Terry is a young jackass who thinks he is a boxer and you taught him different I suppose which is good by me. Terry was in the Navy like me and he was a Navy boxing champ. But don't think for a minute that kid's shenanigans don't go unnoticed. I told him the same thing I'm telling you - no more fighting be it in or out of the ring or you're off my crew."

"Well I appreciate that boss" Cotton says "and I reckon I have no need to fight no more"

and the boss scratches his neck and says

"About the Captain getting his knickers in a twist over you being in town. His daughter used to run with Terry before Terry went into the Navy and so I hear they thought they'd be married and they weren't and the Captain is still sore about all this because Jael is wild and he wants her off his hands. He'd like nothing more than to have Jael marry Terry still but she won't have him and I think I know why. Because he's a brawler and a bully. So steer clear of him and the Captain if you know what's good for you"

Fred Mason says and he is about to shove off when he stops and goes on

"Oh and one last thing I called around in Oregon and dropped your name and they told me you were one hell of a brave man and you saved a man's life and that's how you got the burn on your neck and shoulder during the Tillamook Burn."

"Welllllllll I don't know about all that"

Cotton growled trying to be all modestlike but getting all proud that a man would call on about him and another man would say he is one helluva man.

"Well I do" Mason says and he finishes with "Glad to have you aboard Kingfisher now stay out of damn trouble"

and Cotton stands and watches him go and get into his truck and wave and he thinks he has never met a finer damn Yankee than Fred Mason for Cotton heard Mason came out from the East from a park over there to help run Glacier and Cotton also thinks he has never met a finer damn state than Montana.

Cotton is all fired mad about how Jael was into that Terry kid like Mason told him though he does not know why for it is none of his concern nor business as far as he can figure but he feels it in his gut anyhow. Some people say to follow your nose and some say to follow your heart but Cotton always says to follow your gut because your gut is always hungry and will lead you to the food or some other such thing I don't really know but anyhow he was following his gut where it concerned that girl and it was givin him a gut ache. So he tried to forget all about it for a few weeks while he busted it with Jacob on the crew and they worked so damn hard that Jacob said he was never so tired in all his life but Cotton could tell he liked it because the days went quick and Jacob gained a few pounds of grit n gristle on the work and Cotton's cooking to boot. In all that time Cotton saw the girl a few times in Stumptown but tried to steer clear of her and also that Terry kid who was not bunking in the cabins at the Park thank God but some of his buddies were and they gave Cotton wide berth so to speak. Cotton instead of fighting or mooning over a cottonpickin girl gets all caught up in the Park especially working alongside of Jacob Two Calves who has a spiritual relation with the land like Cotton doesn't being that he is white and not much of a spiritual nature person like the Indians though Jacob makes him want to be one.

Glacier Park is bordered on the West by Flathead River and on the East by the Blackfeet rez like a baby bison layin close to its momma and this is where Jacob comes from is the rez and then right smack dab in the middle of the park the Hump which is what the old hobos called the Continental Divide goes running through just to let you know where you are. There are so many goddang passes like Logan pass and mountains like Chief Mountain and lakes like McDonald's Lake and St. Mary's Lake and Two Medicine Lodge Lake that Cotton can't keep track of em all and he knows he could live here a long time and still see things he aint never seen and he is as happy as a clam about this for he has never been to such a place though he probably has but his eyes were not quite open to what was hanging on the walls if you get my meaning.

If you took the Going to the Sun Road through the

park you would go through some of God's own country being it the Old Man Land Where the World Began and Cotton can't stop rubberneckin at the mountains and pines and lakes and all. The Going to the Sun Mountain is like a ladder to the sky like its own name and Jacob says this is where the Blackfeet used to go for visions from the sun when they came of age and Cotton thinks this is what he needs is a sun vision bygod for he is well past the age when he shoulda gotten one and it aint come yet. All the mountains in the park are like God carved em with his own bare bygod hands and makes Cotton respect God for a bygod hard worker. Jacob tells Cotton about how Old Man rebuilt the world after the flood and how these mountains used to be underwater and then the water went down and took all the sediments and soils and whatnot and spread them all around and then Old Man made people from the soils and Cotton thinks it is mindboggling that man and woman are made from the same stuffs and it makes him think of Jael but he can't bygod so he thinks of something else but he can't so he thinks of her anyways while telling himself that he is not. She becomes the mountains risin up like her breasts and the cliff saddles are the saddles of her hips and the fireweed and beargrass and balsamroot wildflowers are her summer dresses and sometimes Cotton sees her high up like a vision in the sun ridin Going to Sun Mountain like a horse showing a peek of her bare thigh for her dress has rose too high.

He and Jacob go through the Park and clear and raze and shovel and watch for fires on the horizon on lookout towers East and West and there is a few lightning storms that spark a blaze and they go in with a few others and put the blazes down they being just little things and Cotton laughs that he is Smokey the goddang bear as he and Jacob Two Calves the Blackfeet Blood stand in the char leanin on their shovels smokin Cotton's handrolled cigarettes.

17.

On Friday nights over the summer the men on at the Park head to Stumptown for some drinks and maybe a fight and maybe to see a girl which is what they were doing when Cotton caught them in the Dog Leg that day when Cotton first wandered into town but Cotton has been staying away from trouble so he does not go into town so much now but stays in the cabin smokin and drinkin and playing cards with Jacob Two Calves. But this particular Friday night Cotton can't seem to shake being drug into town like that bull drug him the once and bygod he tries not to think he might see that pretty as a glacial plain with elk roamin on it Jael girl but he can't help himself he's a just a man dammit and a Cotton Kingfisher man at that.

Jacob Two Calves goes back to the rez to see his family but before he goes he says

"Don't get into trouble"

and Cotton says

"I am trouble"

and laughs and Jacob knows this but he has become real fond of his buck wild white friend and he would not wish any harm to come to him so he tells him just the same.

Cotton gets to town and tries to do the right thing by avoiding rough places though for the life of him he cannot remember why and he wonders where his bull balls have gone but he don't care all that much truth be told for he is happy in The Land Where the World Began so he heads over to the grange for what he heard was a social from his boss man Fred Mason. Cotton figures Mason is tryin to keep him out of trouble and he likes him for it even though he is a goddamn Yankee they are both fond of another apiece for some reason. Cotton would say the reason why is is that Fred Mason is a good boss and appreciates a hard worker and Fred Mason would say that it is because Cotton is one of the hardest working men he has ever seen but it is more than that and they both know it though neither says it it is just there. That is the way men are sometimes bygod I have seen it they just like one another and some men have a way of pulling another man to em like Cotton to Mason and the other way around. It is a sight to see when you see it a fisher of men like Cotton and I will be damned if this didn't happen to him often the men that he didn't beat gathered around like he was a hobo Jesus dealin out vittles on the mount. Mason did not gather around Cotton for vittles but he respected him just the same as if they'd been in war together and what Cotton did not know is that those men in Oregon not only told Mason about how he saved a man's life in the Tillamook burn but that he also saved a bunch of goddamn men in the War don't ask me how they know this because Cotton don't talk about that so I should just hush up that is his story to tell dammit I only told it for to tell you what Mason heard.

Mason was with his wife when Cotton got there to the grange social and she was one of the prettiest women Cotton has ever seen with fire engine red hair and a poofy skirted flower dress like she was a flower her damn self and she had the manners of an East Coaster but none of the bitch and Cotton dug her like the old negroes say right away.

"I have heard all about you Cotton"

she said and Cotton says

"Well I guess I best be leavin then"

and she and Mason laughed and Mason clapped him on the back like see I told you this guy is somethin else and Cotton felt warm all over because of it and the Mason kids there are three of them one girl and two boys look up at Cotton like he is the toughest goshdarn man they have ever seen with the scars on his arms under his t shirt he is wearing because it is a mite warm and he smiles and winks at them and they smile back like he is a friendly bear.

Cotton feels underdressed in but his white t shirt and new works boots with a white sole and red hide sewn like moccasins for white men for climbing and digging that he bought with his first government paycheck under his rolled up work pants for he realizes it aint just a social it is a goddang square dance party. He tells Mason he shoulda warned him about it bein a dance and Mason says

"You wouldn't have come if I did"

and Cotton has to give him this and also that that Mason is a sly dog.

There is a lantern lit floor laid out behind the grange and a whole mess of townsfolk all who Cotton's reputation has proceeded to and all who cannot believe he is there and with Mason to boot bygod. So Cotton swaggers in like he owns the damn grange just to show the townsfolk it aint no skin off his nose and that he is proud to be with Mason.

Bein that this is a family gathering there aint much to drink but the beer in coolers men bring so Mason shares his beer cans with Cotton and Cotton watches Mason and his wife dance and laugh with the children and he sees those mountains rising up behind them like it is the Mason family's wallpaper and Cotton feels a queer feeling in his bones that he wishes he did not. He never saw his momma and daddy dance and laugh like that and he feels mighty sad about right then and he wonders why Old Man made some men and women from the same good earth and some men and women from the same bad earth. He is standing back guzzlin a beer and watching the dancers and hearing the caller's calls echo off the mountain walls just feeling sad about how his momma and daddy never danced and never laughed when Mrs. Mason Elsa is her name makes Cotton dance with her and the townsfolk are all damned to hell when they see him do all the steps and twirl Mrs. Mason as if he is a goddamn champion square dancer and he might be for I have heard some rumors but I cannot prove them of his dancin days in the Dakotas. Mason and his wife clap when it is all done and then they all sit at a table and eat cold fried chicken Mrs. Mason made up and homemade bread with butter and fruits and berries and beer and cola and the summer night is starting to cool and the light is going Flathead lake blue above the Swan and Rocky Mountains.

"Where did you learn to dance like that?"

Elsa Mason asks him and Cotton says

"I was dancin when I came outta the womb"

and the Mason children giggle and one of the boys the younger one I think says

"Where did you get those scars"

 pointing to Cotton's bare forearms and Mrs. Mason shushes her son and tells him it is not polite to say such things but Cotton says

"The boy is alright ma'am. I earned em every last one of em son. I'll tell you how when you get older"

and the Mason boy looks at his daddy Fred Mason and his daddy nods at him like it would be alright for Cotton to tell him about how he earned them scars every last one of em when the boy is old enough. Cotton remembers how his daddy had scars written upon his flesh but he never told Cotton how he earned them he just let loose their stories by beating them into his son and Cotton would not wish that on any little boy.

Cotton is off by a pine tree alone smokin later in the night when who should he see but that goddamn beautiful Jael girl walk into the lights from the lanterns of the dance floor under the big sky and Cotton's gut heart does an ass over tea kettle so that he coughs on cigarette smoke going down the wrong goozle as his daddy used to say for he was thinking of the girl and not his smoke and she looks over to the coughin and sees him outside the ring of light and smiles and waves at him. She's got a poofy skirt dancin dress like Mrs. Mason and her hair pulled back and red red lips like the color of them New Mexico Blood of Christ Mountains when the sun is goin down that Cotton has not seen for years and years. Cotton don't know if he wants to go into the ring of light as that yonder woman is waving him on in but he is a helluva dancer and she is a helluva girl so he goes back in.

"What are you doing here?"

she asks him nicelike like she is glad he is there just surprised and he says

"Came with the Mason family"

and she says

"Ohhhhh. Getting all domesticated huh?"

and before he can answer Mason comes up and says

"Hello Jael. Cotton remember no trouble you hear?"

and Cotton says

"I don't aim to."

"Oh don't worry" Jael says. "Dad isn't here and neither is Terry. I saw Cotton in the bar that day he beat Terry. Terry was asking for it Mr. Mason."

"Oh I know he was. Cotton here is one of my best men and I couldn't afford to lose him over some trouble about a local thing you know?"

"No problems here"

Jael says

"No problems here"

Cotton says then they are off dancin to a lively tune with Mr. Mason just watching and worrying a touch for he is a wise man that knows about love and knows about trouble and he respects Cotton Kingfisher enough to know that the man is capable of both in spades.

18.

If you have never seen a do si do or a chicken in the breadpan kickin out dough or allemande your partner or promenade or a two step then you are missing out but if you have seen them and haven't seen em done by Cotton then you are further missing out and lastly of all if you have seen either of these things but not with that beer bottle wildflower pretty girl that night under the Montana big sky my friend you missed a show. Cotton was dancin to beat the band and Jael was not to be outdone bygod and they were stepping and kicking and hootin and hollerin and laughing and bygod the townsfolk even got into the show and had to admit the drifter was the best damn dancer they had ever seen. Jael's cheeks were flushed like she was a little girl playin kick the can and Cotton's big sky sun dark skin was shimmering from bustin it like a mule on the dance floor and even though the sun was down Cotton thoughta Old Man smiling down on him. Between dances Jael would sip some punch and pretend to talk to the old ladies or Mrs. Mason while looking at Cotton's fighting crooked profile handsome face above them lady's heads and Cotton would pretend to talk to Fred Mason and the Mason boys but he was watchin Jael the whole time and both of them knew it and both of them liked it bygod. At one point I will be goddamned if Cotton did not pick up a banjo and stiff like at first but better the more oiled up he got bust out an old railroad tune while the old man who's banjo it was clapped him on. Besides that he called two songs for the dancers and he'd call like this

"First couple to the right change and swing change and swing and - mister Peabody put that punch down that's enough now y'hear - change and swing now you're home and everbody swing"

interrupting the dance to call out Mr. Peabody the old banjo man who was drinking punch at the back and everyone would laugh even Mr. Peabody. Jael danced with Mr. Mason and looked up at the rowdy cuss Okie callin from on top of a chair with his accent roaring back though he was not mad at all and she smiled when he winked down at her while she twirled her dress like the wildflowers blooming on the great plains. When the night was wearin thin and the square dance caller was hoarse and the Mason kids were asleep on picnic tables Cotton helped put tables and chairs and children away and some of the elder townsfolk can't remember what they heard about him being such a bad man because they sure had a helluva time with him tonight and you and I both know this is just the way that man can be.

Cotton saw the Masons off with Jael standing at his

side and Mason parted with

"No bruises bumps or scratches on Monday morning Kingfisher"

and Cotton says

"Scouts honor"

and Mrs. Mason smiles at him and Jael like she knows something they don't. Then the ornery mean cuss that is ox bow strong and mule kick tough square dance champ and the big sky big sun made of the mountains girl are standing alone in the dark for a piece and the stars are shining down on them like Christmas lights Cotton has only ever seen from the outside lookin in.

"I can't remember the last time I had that much fun"

Jael says as they lean against his truck and smoke his handrolled cigarettes.

"Me neither"

Cotton says and he means it bygod.

"See you aren't all trouble."

Cotton grunts and says

"I heard bout you and that Terry kid fore I rolled on into town"

for Cotton has never been one to beat about the bush even if it is a fiery bygod bush he figures to just get it outta the way why waste time bygod that's just the way he is and Jael is quiet for a minute smoking after he says this then she goes

 "Yes we were an item"

like they were two cans of beans settin together on the shelf of the grocery store here in town not lovers and this makes Cotton feel a mite better.

"Is that why I haven't seen you?"

she asks.

"Maybe. Or maybe I'm just tryin to stay outta bygod trouble."

"Am I trouble?"

the girl asks and Cotton hears her battin her lashes in the dark.

"If you are with Terry you sure as hell are and your daddy sure as hell don't like me none" and he blows out some smoke then goes on "sides goddamn pretty girls are always trouble"

and he couples the curse to the compliment to make it not seem so goddamn big even though you shouldn't curse in front of a lady but neither should you call her pretty unless you are ready for trouble so he did both at once. Cotton can't see it in the dark but Jael blushes red and not by his cursin which she never minds and she smiles then says

"I am not with Terry anymore and I apologize about my dad. He wanted me and Terry to be something that we aren't. I think he has it out for you because he likes Terry and he is mad at me for not marrying him."

"Whysat? You not marryin and all"

Cotton asks and Jael shrugged.

"It was years ago that Terry and I were an item. Before he went to the Navy. Then he went away for a few years and came back and I was over it but he thought I was still his sweetheart. He isn't the nicest guy and I guess I got sick of him bossing me around. He's a bully and he's been mad ever since I refused him and I guess so has my dad."

"What's your momma say about all this?"

"My mom left my dad a long time ago when I was just a baby. She left to go be a star in California. I don't even know what she looks like. Dad doesn't treat me all that well because of it though he'd never say that. I don't think he likes women too much after mom left. He just wants to marry me off and get me out of the house."

"Damn that is rough sister"

"I'm used to it."

"Your momma musta been real pretty"

Cotton says.

"Why's that?"

"Cause I know you don't get your looks from your daddy"

and Jael likes the compliment very much for it

sounds like an old familiar country and western song especially comin out all rough and smoky Okielike from Cotton.

"You're too much Cotton"

she says and Cotton feels all light as a robin's feather when she says his name familiarlike like they are man and wife at breakfast.

"So Mason thinks you're going to get into trouble?"

Jael asks him.

"Yup he thinks I need to steer clear of just about everyone. I don't blame him I spose he saw Terry after I beat him raw. More n anything Mason don't want me to fail I think."

"Well that's kind of him."

"It sure is now aint it. I don't know if anyone has been kinder to ol Cotton than Mason"

Cotton says and he thinks on this for a bit as he smokes with the girl beside him brushing up against his hot skin like the cool mountain wind.

19.

Now just when the conversation is settling in like the smoke from the cigarettes the couple is shined upon by a pair of headlights and a car stops and the doors swing open and someone gets out and hollers

"Cotton Kingfisher we want to have a word with you!"

and Cotton don't recognize the voice nor the dark figure that owns it but there are five others or more besides luminated in the car headlights like they been drinking muddy water for Cotton cant make none of them out.

"Y'all come back for another ass whoopin"

Cotton hollers and Jael looks very scared but Cotton just laughs.

"Get away from the girl" the voice says "We know what your intentions are"

and when the stranger says this he gives Cotton a sudden notion that they aim to harm Jael and blame it on the drifter the drifter bein him so Cotton says real quick

"Get in the truck n lock it"

then he shoves Jael into the truck cab as someone comes at him from the dark swingin a goddamn baseball bat whooshin through the air but Cotton dodges it and it busts the truck with a sound like a shell off a tank turret and Cotton picks up whoever swung that goddamn bat bodily by the throat and groin and heaves him up and over the truck clean to the other side and Cotton hears whoever it is screaming as he is sailin through the air. Another jackass tries to reach the truck door where Jael is hiding but she slams the lock and Cotton sees red though it is black outside and drives his fist so hard into the man's face goin for the door that it breaks that man's jaw with a crack like snap and the man just slobbers and slumps and the fight is over for him as he drops like a bag of bygod flour to the dust but Cotton catches a bat hard clean across his back and he is mad now whooooo boy watch out he turns quick as a big horn sheep on Grinnell Glacier and head butts the bat bearer in the throat as he catches another bat hard across his ribs as the man he head butts falls back like a mover's dolly stacked with boxes back down some stairs and Cotton gets hit again with a damn bat and he can't quite see who all is where but what he can do is grab the bat as it whistles in at him and he does exactly that he catches a blow in his callous mitt palm and with wrench wrist strength yanks the bat out of one of the hands of one of those bastards and as another comes in on him he blocks it with his own procured timber and throws off the blow then brings his bat up and cleaves back down like he is bringing an axe down on Oregon timber and it drops someone right quick no cry or nothin he hit the poor SOB so hard. Someone on the passenger side of the truck hits Jael's window hard and it breaks in on her as she screams and Cotton blocks a homerun hit and runs and leaps into the back of the truck and out to the other side with a goddamn bre'r rabbit bound and as he flies through the air he slashes his bat down on the window breaker so hard that he breaks the man's bat as he tries to protect himself with it and Cotton's bat keeps on goin and breaks the man's shoulder from his chest cage as well as his bat and the man is outta the fight hollerin and cryin in the dirt. There is a scurry from the attackers as the car roars to life and starts to drive on off into the night and some of the men are left and start chasing after it shouting and Cotton chases after them and Jael from the locked truck has never seen a man so fast as this he chases down one man and clobbers him from behind and still has time to go after another and this man is in trouble for Cotton is so mad he hits him several times with a bat then get this he takes this man over his shoulder and throws him up into a tree bygod I swear and I will be damned if that man does not stick up in there.

Only then is Cotton done.

A few others managed to get away so Cotton is angry as all hell and he does not even care that he won as he hears nothing but blood in his ears pounding like a damn Blood war drum. From the truck Jael can see his crooked fighting profile in the headlights of the truck and his white shirt gleaming white with specks of blood here and there on it and he is just standing there his chest heaving up and down in the swirling dust with his arms clenched like pine boughs. She stays in the truck not unlocking the doors and she wonders why these men hate this man so much and what is going on in Stumptown and bygod this man is one helluva brawler. She sees Cotton light up a cigarette and start to smoke and though she is a little scared of him she wishes he would get back on in the truck with her. What she does not know and it is probably better that she don't is that Cotton is waiting for the bloodrush to calm down for he feels like he could kill someone if he aint careful it wouldn't be the first time bygod but it would be the first time he has let the bloodrush go away without trying to squeeze it out like a tube of toothpaste so he lets it. By the time he heads back to the truck and clambers in he has finished a smoke and started another and he asks Jael

"Y'alright girl"

and she says

"Yes my god are you?"

and he says

"Uh huh"

then starts the truck and drives off leaving the clobbered men just layin around in the dust near the grange and one of them still hangin up in a tree like a bar brawl crucifix.

"They must want me out bad if they'd harm you"

Cotton says on the way back to Jael's house.

"They weren't going to harm me" she says "They just wanted to scare me."

"Honey them boys aint messin around. They want me outta town and they were gonna do somethin to you and pin it on me I heard it."

Cotton drives Jael to her daddy's house who is not there and she says

"Come on in and I'll see to you"

pointin to welts forming on him from the bat blows he took and he says

"Sugar I aint gonna get arrested by your daddy for being violent"

and Jael says

"You didn't do anything but in self defense dammit!"

and Cotton says

"You think that matters cause it don't and sides I'm fine"

and Jael gets all mad that he is acting like it aint nothin when it is something and he don't have to act so damn tough in front of her she saw how hard he got hit so she hollers

"Cotton Kingfisher you shut your mouth and get

inside so I can see to you right this minute!"

and no girl talks to Cotton Kingfisher like that bygod but she just did so Cotton yes ma'ams and goes on into the house and lets her see to him bygod. He takes his bloody t shirt off and sits on the edge of the bathtub in the bathroom of an old house in Stumptown with yellow painted walls and pictures of birds and some paintings of landscapes and such. Jael runs some water and gives him ice cubes wrapped in kitchen towels and uses witch hazel on the welts and bruises now running fresh stories over his calloused hide. He does not wince once as she sees to him just smokes and she thinks he is the toughest bygod man she has ever seen and she respects him for it as only a woman could for men see Cotton as an ornery cuss but being she is a woman she is able to see him as a brave man who has seen too much to tell by lettin on by wincing at a little ol thing like witch hazel. He sits there and smokes while Jael soaks his bruisings and he looks at a painted picture of Going to the Sun Mountain with a sunset behind it like you'd climbed the ladder and found the sun and now the sun could say goodbye.

"There's a pretty picture"

he says as he looks at it and Jael says

"Thanks."

"Did you do it?"

Cotton asks and he turns to the girl nursing on him.

148

"Yes."

"You paint? Damn sister that is alright. I see that mountain everday and you really nailed it."

"Thanks Cotton"

and he likes the way she says his name all familiarlike like they are a married couple gettin ready for to go to bed together.

"I'd no idea you're an artist."

"Yeah I dabble. I like to paint and draw. Landscapes mostly. I also do some pottery."

"No kiddin? That's real fine Jael real fine"

and Jael likes the way he says her name instead of callin her girl and honey and sugar and missy like he is her husband and she is patching him up from a hard day working the big raw boned earth.

20.

While Jael is soaking his wounds she touches some of his scars so as he wont know but she touches them to know his story and she feels something inside her at all those scars especially the Tillamook burn one and she touches it tender like she wishes she could heal it all up. At some point while Jael is nursing and touching barechested Cotton the police captain comes home to find his one and only daughter patching up the goddamn slaughterhouse drifter in his own bygod bathroom with yellow walls and pictures of birds and landscapes and his head nearly explodes for Cotton has seen a man's head explode bygod though he does not ever want to discuss it and it looks pretty close to the way the Capn's head is gettin.

"What in the hell is going on here"

the captain shouts and he aint askin he is tellin and Jael acts like nothing is going on here and stands and brushes past her daddy and they go into the kitchen and there is a big shouting match wherein she tells her daddy how men tried to abuse her and blame Cotton and he won't believe it. Cotton stays in the bathroom a piece just smoking and lookin at that pretty picture Jael painted all by herself then he throws his shirt over his shoulder and heads out the door stopping in the kitchen doorway to say

"I better head back Jael thankee for your kineness"

and she says

"You don't have to go"

and he says

"The hell I don't"

pointing at her daddy's gun on his belt and the Capn looks all offendedlike like how dare you say I would shoot an unarmed man I am a damn officer of the goddamn law but he and Cotton both know that Cotton is the most dangerous unarmed man they have ever seen and that damn officer of the goddamn law has the prettiest daughter in all the mountains so all bets are off.

"I'm not done with you yet Kingfisher"

the captain hollers after him but Cotton don't give a damn as he is done and when he is done he is gone and he is done so he is gone don't matter the man tellin him he aint done. He climbs in the truck and heads on back to the cabin and drinks whiskey and gets hard drunk all alone but not before he barricades the doors and windows just in case and wraps himself in his Indian blanket his favorite possession and drifts off to the big rock candy going to the sun mountains with Jael ridin them like a painted pony on the Plains.

Monday at roll call Fred Mason is missing some of his crew and Terry is jitterylike like he had too much coffee and cigarettes and Cotton is sore as all hell but he won't let on bygod so Mason says nothing as he hands out jobs and they set to work. Cotton wants to give Terry a smile from ear to ear which Cotton knows from his daddy means to slit his throat for hiring men to come and beat him and not coming himself but he wants to keep his Land Where the World Began job so he bides his time and this may be the first time this has ever happened to him that he knows of.

The Stumptown folks are all talking about a bloody mess of a fight at the grange after the dance and Cotton hears somehow that he had left by then so it could not have been him and he is mighty obliged to Jael for not spillin the beans though he never needed no woman to stick up for him and he wonders how she is keeping her daddy's tin star yap shut. Cotton tells Jacob Two Calves about the whole thing and Jacob says

"You should be careful. It sounds like they want you out bad"

and Cotton says

"Dammit son they can't chase me outta the Land Where the World Began no sir just let em try bygod"

and Jacob is afraid for he knows they will try again and he worries for his wild white friend for Jacob is earthwise and knows the darkness like a dog gone bad waiting to bite that lays in all men's hearts be they red or white.

Cotton and Jacob work on a landslide area in the mountains digging away and Cotton hears an injun shaker rattlesnake too late and that cottonpickin sidewinder takes a swipe at him but it glances off of Cotton's brand new stiff work pants and Jacob shouts for him to look out and Cotton jumps up and sideways like he was in a goddang cartoon and lands a few feet away from that winder but get this even Jacob is amazed when Cotton don't run but goes after that bygod rattler and reaches real quicklike behind and grabs it by the tail and snaps it up then brings it down like a bullwhip cracking crushing its head on a rock. Jacob is a little rattled no pun intended but Cotton just smiles and holds up the snake and hollers

"Well I guess we know what's for supper"

and it was bygod.

What Jacob didn't know and what I am tellin you now is that his wild white friend has always been snake catchin crazy and some men say this is from his daddy beating on him that made him wild like that and some men say his daddy beat on him on account of his being wild like that but I suppose it is both and neither for Cotton was always just walleyed buck wild. He would catch snakes like that there rattler with his bare hands as a boy goddamn copperheads I tell you while his little brother clambered up into a tree and hollered down at him

"Goddangit Cotton daddy is gonna whoop you"

but Cotton didn't care none bygod and he'd keep handling them there snakes. Cotton would keep them cottonpicking copperheads in a crate cage he made until once his drunk ass daddy found them out and I will be damned if his drunk ass daddy did not grab a copperhead by its tail just like his son Cotton but he was not catchin he was killin and he slung it up against a tree like a whip just like Cotton did with that there rattler busting its skull. Cotton would get powerful angry at his daddy in those times and pray to God that the snakes would bite him and kill him deader n a doornail but they never did and this is one of the reasons Cotton has an aggrievance with God for God never answered even that simplest little prayer.

Jacob Two Calves made a necklace for Cotton from the rattle of the rattler on a leather string and he said it would bring Cotton good luck and also they could use it to find out if there was other rattlers about when they were in the rocks and this is why Cotton wears that rattler necklace on his neck to this day.

Mason stops by the cabin later that week and asks if Cotton is ok and if he was involved in the grange fight though he knows goddamn good and well he was by the list of injuries such as broken jaws and shoulders unhinged from chest cages and a goddamn man hanging in a tree like a bar brawl crucifix and Cotton says

"Do y'want the truth or the not truth"

155

and Fred Mason says

"Neither dammit. But Cotton I like you so be careful. I can't figure out why captain Carter hasn't bothered me about it being as you're all my employees but he hasn't. But stay out of trouble now you hear"

and Cotton says he does hear and Mason tells Jacob Two Calves to keep his eye on the fireline Okie and Jacob says nothing but nods his head and Cotton says to Mason to tell the family hi and after Mason goes Cotton laughs but Jacob doesn't so Cotton says

"Why so down in the mouth brother"

but Jacob Two Calves won't say so they play cards and drink buck whiskey then sleep in their Indian blankets but Jacob barricades the door and windows just in case.

Not two days later as Cotton and Jacob are playing cards tryin to stay outta trouble like Mason told them they hear a car pull up and they hide their whiskey but not their cards and someone knocks on the cabin door and Cotton sees that beautiful dancing Jael girl through the screen and his heart gets going like a jackhammer and he would know he's run them in the cities for he is always the strongest man on the crew.

"You better get inside fore Mason sees you"

Cotton says and he pulls her inside even though it aint really proper and Jacob Two Calves says he will go out for an evening stroll and I will be damned if he didn't though I will tell you this and not Cotton

156

is that Jacob went a piece from the cabin and hid in the trees and watched the cabin and smoked to look out for his buck white friend.

Standin there together in the cabin a little too close Cotton thinks Jael smells like wildflowers and the sun and Jael thinks Cotton smells like the smoky earth and the weavings of whiskey and this suits both of them just fine so they stand too close quiet like this for a bit gettin high off eachother's fumes.

21.

"I brought you something"

Jael says and hands Cotton a brown paper bag package and Cotton says

"Whatsis?"

"Open it"

Jael replies so he opens it and it is a rustic pottery coffee mug but fired all nice and glossy with a deep blue sky color going brown and it reminds Cotton of them mountains all around and Jael says

"It's a coffee mug I made for you. Do you like it?"

and it means the world to Cotton that she gave him this here mug for no one has given him anything so kind as something they made with their own bare hands especially a woman especially such a pretty one at that and he imagines her slender pretty fingernail painted fingers workin the mug into something he will put to his mouth every day and he nearly can't speak but he can so he says

"That's mighty nice of you and good work too"

"I told you I did pottery. There is a sun and such on it for The Land Where the World Began like you are always going on about and your name too."

"That is somethin to see Jael girl I don't think I ever got a nicer gift"

and Jael is happy for she sees that he means what he says though he is trying to be a man about it and she don't care if he is a man about it dammit just as long as he likes it and she can see he does like it.

Cotton makes up some coffee and they sit at the table and have some black joe with whiskey and it is oh so smooth but stout enough it'll put hair on your chest and Cotton stares at this girl for she's pretty in a red scarf in her hair and denim jeans and a work shirt with rolled up sleeves showing bronzed arms all speckled with clay like she just came fresh from throwing his mug and Going to the Sun Woman Jael starts to look mighty fine finer that usual which is a lot bygod I will tell you and I know that this is the prettiest girl Cotton has ever seen.

"How come no one has come to raise cane on me since the grange brawl"

Cotton asks the girl and she says

"I lit into my dad about the town being crooked and all. He was mad about it but what could he do he couldn't call me a liar and I spread the word I got jumped and you saved me. Dad had to go clean up the whole thing. I think he might be seeing the light of day in all this and that you're not so bad after all."

"Well I'm mighty obliged to you for stickin up for me not that I need it bygod"

"Of course not"

Jael says with a smile and Cotton goes on

"But I'll believe that when I see it bout your daddy"

"He went and talked to Terry and Terry said he didn't have anything to do with it"

"That dog don't hunt with me that lil runt"

Cotton goes off and Jael laughs and he has never had someone laugh at his being angry so he sips his whiskey coffee and smacks his lips and says

"Well I'm serious bygod that little liar if he comes near me I will kill him with my bare hands sohelpmegod"

"Why haven't you killed him with your bare hands yet?"

Jael asks and Cotton says

"I don't know I guess I reckon I like this place and I like this job and the earth has been pretty kind to me around here and I don't wanna make no trouble for boss Mason he's been real good to me"

"That's pretty big for a cuss like you"

Jael says and she smiles white teeth and all and Cotton crooked grins in spite of himself for she is teasin him and he aint never liked being teased but she has always been able to get away with it since the day he first laid eyes on her big sky big sun faded red dress in the Dog Leg.

"The people in town are all talking about you" she goes on "about the dance and how you were such a hoot."

"Are they? Well I'll be a monkey's uncle"

"I think that's part of it is the town is starting to turn in your favor"

"I can't figure why"

"There's just something about you Cotton"

Jael smiles and Cotton likes the way she says this like there really is something about him that would make people be on his side when he has always been the outsider.

"Even the minister was talking about you"

"The hell you say"

"Yes" and Jael laughs at his expressionism "he was talking about you being a smart man or something but maybe a bit touchy"

then Cotton goes on about how that sweet little minister character is always sneakin up behind him as he minds his own business on the church bench and Jael finds it amusing and he tells her about how the rattler tried to kill him the other day when she asks about his necklace and he asks her about pottery and Montana and painting. They talk and talk about nothin and Cotton has never really cared about a woman so much to talk and talk about nothin no disrespect to all the others and Cotton would mean no disrespect to them but this is just the truth. Then they head out for Jael to get back in her car and go home and she says

"I am sorry I misjudged you"

and he says

"Didja"

and she says

"Yes when you first came into town. Maybe I'd have thought different about you if you and Terry had a square dancing contest instead of a boxing match that day"

and Cotton curses at the ridiculous idea and she says

"Oh I wanted to tell you about the sun on your mug I made you. Inside of the sun there is a warclub and a peacepipe that's what those things are in case you were wondering"

and he wasn't but he is now and she says

"You know because you are a warrior who is making peace with the earth"

and Cotton thinks this sounds like what the minister said to him that one day but it does not make him angry this time it makes so much goddamn horse

163

sense that he looks down on big sky big moon yonder woman Jael standing right in front of him and he does something he aint never and it is that he leans down and kisses Jael on her neck under her jawbone that runs graceful like the deer upon the plains even though it aint proper and he hears her catch a breath like a trout out of water when he does this and his cheek rasps hers then he says

"goodnight"

and turns and goes back inside. It is awhile before Jael's car starts up then she is gone and when Jacob Two Calves comes back in the cabin he finds Cotton lying on his back on his bed staring up at the ceiling and Jacob says

"Goodnight Cotton Kingfisher"

and Cotton says

"G'night Jacob Two Calves"

and they sleep in peace.

22.

There is a small fire in the North mountains that Jacob and Cotton go to put out by taking a rough service road and come down on top of it and cut it off before it gets out of hand. It is big enough a blaze that they need several crews and Terry and his boys are workin it and Cotton is in charge of them all.

Cotton is heaving and hacking and sweating in the Old Man big sun in the big heat of the blaze shirtless and shining though he is not supposed to be shirtless he don't care none because it is hotter n Old Blickeys and his shirt bout rubs him raw. So Cotton is heaving and hacking and he gets mighty bothered that when he looks on down the line he sees that Terry kid busting it like a mule with him and he gets mad he has to share a line with that pissant but there is nothing to be done for it. When they have beat the fire and they stand in the char smokin Cotton gets all fired up and goes over to Terry and his crew though Jacob tells him no. Terry stands when he sees Cotton coming for no man wants to be sitting when Cotton Kingfisher is on top of you and besides he looks like a bronze scarred big sun god shining shirtless comin through the smoke. Terry throws his chest out and Cotton marches up right in front of him and Terry is taller than he Cotton aint too tall just under six feet and Terry is just over but they both know who is bygod stronger and it isn't the tallest man standin on this charred strip of mountain flesh.

"Nice work today kid"

Cotton says and Terry is a bit surprised and he says

"Thank you"

though his jawbone is clenched like a snapped wolf trap and Cotton goes on

"Nicer than when you sent your boys to shit me up. I know you tried to kill me and hurt the girl and pin it on me that night after the dance you little shit"

and Terry flinches and his eyebrow twitches and his crew pick up their shovels like weapons but they also back away but Terry says

"I don't know what you are talking about"

and Cotton says

"The hell ya don't bygod don't piss down my back and call it rain"

and the mountain goes quiet as a goddamned grave not even a bird is singin now and the smoke is still risin up a bit and the big sky sun is hell hot and it feels like they are in the devil's half acre and he goes on

"Let me tell you somethin boy - if you think that boxing match was bad ya aint seen what I can dish out bygod unless I guess you did you saw your boys put in the hospital by me"

and Terry says

"I don't know what you mean Mr. Kingfisher"

real loudlike so the others will hear him but it is warbly scared and no one gives a good goddamn they wish Terry would just run and not bring the house down on them with himself.

"The hell you don't you little shit. Don't ever come near me again y' hear"

and Terry is standing up straight like he stood up straight in the Navy starin past Cotton's shoulder like he stared over his officer's shoulder in the Navy and Cotton finishes

"and stay away from the girl"

then Terry loses his cool Lord love him though the men around him try to shush his fool damn mouth while he shouts

"Who the hell do you think you are? You stay away from her you old bull"

and Cotton just turns and walks off through the black land as Terry shouts after him and the others try to shut up his fool damn mouth.

"She isn't yours! You stay away from her!"

Terry yells as Cotton and Jacob drive off in the truck and Jacob reaches over and rattles the rattler rattle on Cotton's neck and Cotton lets him and Jacob does it and Cotton doesn't ask why and Jacob never says why but they both know why.

Cotton stands outside the cabin and smokes and he feels the wind is startin to blow fire season Blackfeet wind in full bloom but what about after the fire season work is over where will he go and he does not know. He has not even thought about wandering for a long while and he cannot believe himself for this and he almost gets riled at himself but then he doesn't bygod cause he is happier n a hog on ice here and he don't know if he has ever been happy just high like a kite in the wind that will always come down but right now he feels like a jet plane tearin up above just lookin down all content with a full belly and a happy heart. He thinks on his family and for the first time not really but the first time he will admit it to himself he thinks he wishes he could bust it like a mule on the same line with his little brother and he thinks about him and his brother and Jacob Two Calves bustin it on the same line sweatin together then looking up at one another with smoke smudged faces and smilin for life is good. He also thinks that he and Jael would be married and they would go to the Mason's and all the children would play and he and Mason would drink beer and wrestle the children and his brother then he would go home and lay next to Jael in a bed he bought with his government money that

168

he earned himself with his own damn hands and she would be warm and in a frilly get up and here is where the dream sorta breaks down into Jael sexy thoughts. I will leave those thoughts for Cotton for you bygod know those thoughts are sacred even to Cotton whose story I am telling for I aint tryin to tell it all like those thoughts of Jael but I bet they were beautiful thoughts for she is a goddamn beautiful woman that Old Man made from the Montana earth and rib of man. She is so pretty Cotton figures when he thinks of her that it aches like the ache of a bullet in the body and Cotton would know for he has had a bullet in the body and she aches like that only on the end of the ache there is sweet pain like whiskey not like his real bullet holes that just ache on cold nights n rainy days. Cotton does not know this but I do and I am sure you do too by now that Jael plucks his strings and not the mean ones just the good ones and she has set them to hummin from head to heart to rib.

On the weekend Jacob goes home to the rez to see his family but before he goes he says

"Don't get into trouble"

and Cotton says

"I am trouble"

and they always say that but Cotton is joking and Jacob Two Calves is not or I guess neither of them is joking now that I come to think of it.

Cotton heads on down to a lake where there is a touristy lodge and where Mason is bringing his family for a picnic so Cotton heads on down with a cooler full of beer and hamburgers and whatnot and he finds the Masons down by the lake picnicking like a buncha sun children not a care in the bygod world. Elsa Mason is a mighty fine woman in her yella swimsuit and campfire red hair and sunglasses and bare white shoulders and long white legs and Fred Mason is a handsome devil in Navy swimtrunks and the kids are looking happy and sunbaked and when Cotton comes up they call him Mister Cotton and he likes it for it aint too formal. There are other locals and campers and tourists down at the beach and it is one fine damn party in the sun but the water is so glacier cold it grabs you by the balls and won't let go and the Mason boys run back and forth jumpin in then runnin out and toweling off and Mason and Cotton laugh at them and drink beer while Elsa lies on a towel and reads her magazines. After a few beers Cotton hops on into the water and whoooeee boy it is colder n a welldigger's ass but he dares the boys to stay in with him and they do bygod while Fred watches from the shore and Cotton picks up the boys and throws them and they splash down like incoming shells in the water and come up laughing and coughing for it is so cold. Cotton is careful with the boys for their slippery limbs feel so fragile he fears he will break them and he wonders if he was this brittle as a boy and if so how did his daddy not break him though he guessed he did. Then Mason comes in and he's a goddamn Navy man so he skims under the water like a torpedo then grabs Cotton's leg and they wrassle a bit in play for Mason knows Cotton can beat the everloving hell out of him but he wants to show the man he is his friend and not

170

an enemy and Cotton likes it bygod like wrasslin with his little brother and he takes it easy on his friend boss. Then the boys head back into the shore and Cotton and Mason stay up to their chests and look up at the mountains that feed the lake with glacier water and both men wonder though neither man says what will become of them for this is what them big sky mountains do to a man's thoughts. Then Elsa calls em back on in for burgers and beer and they grapple one another some more and the kids laugh when Cotton picks Mason up and drags him back to shore and Mason shouts

"I let him do that"

and the kids say it aint so and Cotton winks at em for they all know it aint. The little Mason girl goes and brings Cotton an extra towel for he didn't bring his own he is that callous skinned bygod and he is much obliged by her kindness and the kindness of this family and maybe bygod just maybe the kindness of mankind for if little ones are so kind to a broke down mean old ornery cuss drifter like himself then maybe there is hope for the rest of us all dear Lord.

23.

Cotton's mouth is flyin open every time he bends his elbow as he is eating and yapping at the table as the kids play near the water when he hears Elsa Mason say

"My my will you look at that"

and he looks up to see who do you bygod think Jael Carter the Stumptown police captain's daughter switchhippin on out to the lake with a few of her girlfriends in a damn stripy bathing suit of all things with her bare shoulders and her gams glistening and Fred Mason says

"Are you kidding me how does that girl always know where this man is"

as if he has tried his damndest but God just aint helping him out here and Cotton goes tongue tied and the damndest thing is that he stands up from the picnic table as if he is standin to attention and Mason says

"Sit down and stay out of trouble"

and Elsa says

"Fred she is the prettiest girl around I don't know how you expect him to stay away from that" as she nods at Jael's switchhipping and smiles because she likes the idea of love and she loves her husband and she can see her husband likes the Cotton man a great deal though he is rougher n a cob and this makes her love her husband even more for liking such a man and sticking up for him so and she thinks my wouldn't it be lovely to get Cotton and Jael all hitched up. So she is planning out a wedding before Jael even sees them all for that is just the way women are and you and I both know it bygod.

"At least play it cool"

Fred gives in just a bit and Cotton sits down like the boss is right and Mason hands him a beer to hide behind but goddamnit Elsa waves Jael on over and Mason just shakes his head like he don't like the order but he's obeying it like his Navy days. Jael sees em and she brings a couple of younger girls over to the table and they aint nothin compared to her in her stripy bathing suit with bare brown shoulders and a hint of breasts sweet Lord and those legs and hips and her black hair pulled back in a band that matches her suit. Cotton wants to mime like he is shaking a salt shaker on his hand then bite his hand like it is a steak like he has seen the old hobos do when they see a pretty girl but he knows this is not the right thing to do especially after he kissed this girl's neck like a honeybee to honeysuckle so he just squints up at her into the big sun from where he is sittin next to Fred at a picnic table like a roughneck and swigs his beer barechested and says

"Hey girl"

and it comes off a little smoky sexy to the rest of everyone and they wonder if somethin has happened between these two and Old Man Up Above which we all know has but they don't so we don't tell either that's Cotton's tale to tell and Jael's tale as well I guess and I know this is Cotton's story but I am kinda partial to Jael myself like a sister if you must know.

"Hi"

Jael says sweet like honey the bee makes after the honeysuckle and now everyone really is wonderin what in the hell happened between these two and Old Man Up Above the local girl and the mean cuss rowdy ass violent bull mule ballbreaker drifter then Fred Mason jumps in

"Come down for a swim? The water is nice"

"Yes if you like ice cubes"

says Elsa and the girls laugh.

"I like your bathing suit"

Elsa says to Jael bygod calling attention to her amazing form on purpose Cotton and Mason both think and Jael gets all kinda bashful and says

"Oh thank you I made it myself"

and Cotton takes a gander and he will be damned she sure is good with her hands she does it all and

Fred Mason sorta nudges him like don't poke your eye out but Cotton thinks Mason is tellin him to speak up so he speaks up

"Damn that's good work sugar it fits you like a glove"

and Jael's friends giggle and Elsa raises her eyebrows and Mason rubs his hand over his mouth and jaw and Jael blushes and says

"Why thank you Cotton"

and Cotton can see everyone is wonderin what to say next and he don't give a damn for that bathing suit runs right along her curves like the Going to the Sun Road runs right along the mountains sleek and smooth and you gotta take that road slow or else you'll topple over the edge and he is proud of Jael for making that suit like it was no damn thing just like her paintings and that mug what she made him so he says

"Wanna beer"

and she says

"Sure thanks"

and he grabs one from the cooler and church keys it for her and it cracks open on him and he hands it to her and their fingers touch on the ice cold glacier can and he folds his brawny ass oak arms over his barechest and watches her take a drink.

"You girls can lay out here if you'd like" Elsa says "I've got a lot of magazines and I need some feminine company after these two" and nods at

Fred and Cotton.

"Thanks a lot"

Cotton jokes and Elsa says

"Oh Cotton it was a compliment. You're like ten men"

and now he gets a bit bashful and Mason says

"Let's go get in the water Samson it's hotter than hell around here"

and he does not mean because of the big sky big sun so he and Cotton take fresh beers into the lake and stand with their balls under the water drinking beer and tryin not to shiver. Jael's friends lay out with Elsa but Jael don't of course as Fred Mason says but she just bygod wades hip switch wide out into the lake after Fred and Cotton making the water ripple out away from her hips and she brings her beer with like it aint nothin well hell she aint got nuts to freeze off Cotton thinks but he admires her spunk just the same.

"How's it going out here?"

she asks and Fred says

"Amazing. I love this place. Jael how long you lived here?"

"All my life."

"Y'ever think about leavin?"

Cotton asks and she shakes her head

"No. This is The Land Where the World Began"

and Cotton knows she is talkin just to him though Fred Mason don't.

"Has Terry Clay been bothering you?"

Fred asks her a sudden and Cotton is surprised by this though he likes that Mason just comes on out and bygod asked it and he respects his boss friend Fred Mason and Jael says

"He's tried to talk to me a few times"

"About Cotton?"

"About the whole thing yeah."

"I think you should stay away from him if you're hanging out with Cotton" Fred says. "They don't have a whole lot of love for each other and I'd hate to see this place wrecked and lose a good man if you get my meaning"

and Cotton can see he's trying to appeal to the girl's sensitivities and he would be angry with another man for talkin about him so to a girl while he stands right there but it is Fred Mason and he likes Fred Mason a great deal goddamn yankee or no so he don't care none.

"I understand Fred" Jael says "I guess I just don't like Terry bullying me about what I can and can't do"

"That makes a lot of sense just be careful I like the both of you mighty fine" then Mason wades back to shore with "I'm freezing me lower extremities off"

and when he gets back to shore he sits by Elsa and watches the two in the water and he worries just a touch for he knows what not everyone else does is the men he called in Oregon said not only was Cotton good at saving men in the Tillamook Burn and the War but he also was real good at killin em as well when push came down to goddamn shove.

24.

Cotton and Jael swim in the glacier water like it aint even cold because they don't bygod feel it and Elsa Mason would say it's because those two are melting the whole damn glacier and she fans herself to make the point but Mason says to bygod cut it out he gets it already. Big sky crow girl's wet carmel skin with hints of white in all the right places is almost too much for ol Cotton and likewise she likes his bare wet scarred big sun smelling skin as well so they flirt in the water and graze limbs beneath the surface of the lake even when the Mason kids come out to play with them and Cotton thinks it might be fine to have a Jael wife in Montana with Montana children and work fires in the summer and snow in the winter and Jael thinks it might be nice to have a Forest Service husband who aint Terry Clay and who is Cotton Kingfisher and have little Cotton cusses and play in the lakes in the summer and stay indoors in the winter. At one point Cotton grabs that girl's waist under the water to tease her and she don't push him away and his bustin hands stay on the saddles of her hips on her wet stripy homemade bathing suit and if it weren't for the bein in broad daylight not that Cotton usually cares about that sorta thing they'd of kissed hard and maybe more. He runs his roughstock thumbs along the edge of her hips through the bathing suit and Jael looks right into his diamond eyes with her Flathead lake blue eyes as he does this and it is the most beautiful pain Cotton Kingfisher has ever known to have a girl look into him so. Then Jael rides piggyback on him in the water chasing them Mason children though this aint proper and Cotton feels her wet breasts and thighs against him and he fears she will hear his heart in his chest going like a jackhammer that he worked in the city because he is always the strongest man on the crew.

"Let's swim across the lake"

Jael says after a bit and Cotton says

"Damn girl that's a long ways"

and she says

"You chicken?"

and this is all he needs and he starts swimming like his old lifeguard days across the cold blue mountain run off. He busts it breaststroke with his head down like he aint never and the water is in his ears and nose bubblin up and he catches a glimpse of the mountains as he comes up and goes back down and he realizes he is in deep dark knife cold water and he is halfway out to nowhere. He thinks war in the water thoughts though the water then was warm and he thinks of his momma down below

182

him lookin up with animal sad eyes and he loses his steam and stops and treads water tryin to get his air. He can see Jael coming up behind him strong and he is panting like a dog tired dog and it is from the water thoughts and he does not want to look down because hells bells it is come to Jesus deep and God knows what is down there maybe even his momma. Jael sees him and pulls up and treads water and Cotton hollers at her

"Let's head on back"

"Fine chicken let's race"

and Jael heads back and Cotton catches a nice shot of her backside headin back and he lets her beat him back for he likes her backside in that bathing suit and he aint got the spunk no more to bust it back after them water thoughts caught him like a shiv up under the ribs. They come out of the water close to one another and Cotton is done with this damn charade of not touching her he feeling raw nerved from his rib shiv water thoughts like why would the earth do that to me when I was just gettin a head of steam so he puts his arm around Jael's bare shoulders and Jael nestles up under his brawny arm and she doesnt know anything was wrong.

Jael's girlfriends head out and the Masons pack up while Jael and Cotton stand in their towels hemmin n hawin not wanting to leave off just yet and Cotton gets all moroselike like he won't ever get to see Jael's Garden of Eden curves in that dripping like water from the glaciers running into the lake stripy bathing suit again bygod.

As the Masons leave the children say goodbye to the friendly bear and Mason says to Cotton

"You want to come home with us?"

and Cotton says

"No"

though he knows Mason is trying to keep him out of Jael trouble and Elsa says

"Jael you should come out real soon and we could have Cotton over and have a barbeque"

and Fred Mason rubs his mouth and jaw like it's an order he don't want to obey but he is obeying it bygod just like his Navy days and Jael says

"That sounds lovely"

and Elsa says

"I'll telephone you"

then stands on her tiptoes and kisses Cotton on the cheek and says

"Thanks for being sweet to the children and putting up with my husband. Oh and I don't think you're a bad man at all I don't see what all the fuss is about"

and Cotton feels kind of sensitivelike like the earth really does love him damn them water thoughts and Elsa is a sweet redheaded American lake spirit that is telling him the earth loves him and he wants to cry like Elsa is his momma sister but he don't he just kisses her back on the cheek and thanks her then Mason punches his shoulder and shakes his hand and says

"I'll see you on Monday Bull. Jael keep him out of trouble will you"

and she says of course she will what else then Jael and Cotton are left on the lake shore in towels and wet suits and the big sun is headed down toward the big mountains to bed down for the night.

"What now?"

Jael asks and Cotton is glad she does for he thought she might want to go home and he says

"Let's go on up to the Lodge and I'll buy you dinner"

and she says

"Like a date?"

and he is sick of this damn dumb charade so he says

"Hell yeah sister"

and she likes his swagger so she says

"But I don't have anything to wear"

and he says

"That's the best part"

and she don't even try to act scandalized she just laughs and says

"Oh my"

real sassylike and Cotton says

"I got my t shirt you can throw that on"

and she says

"What will you wear?"

"Well I got a workshirt in the truck"

so they go to the Lodge restaurant looking like bygod hoodlums Jael still showin her amazing legs under Cotton's white t shirt Cotton don't wanna call them gams in his mind no more for it seems a cryin shame to disrespect em so and Cotton looks goddamn ridiculous in his cut off work pant shorts and bare legs and unlaced work boots and a work shirt over his bare chest with his rattlesnake rattler necklace and his hair kinda crazy like but not too crazy for he fixed it with the comb in the truck because he don't like his hair outta place like we know. The people in the restaurant are a little put off because it is a pretty nice place bein a tourist trap and all and Cotton wonders why the hell men are wearin suit jackets when they are supposed to be camping bygod but they are. Some of the workers to whom Cotton's reputation has proceeded as a buck hard worker lead him and Jael to a nice table and there is even a candle lit and they sit down lookin water fresh like American Indian Glacier blue lake spirits.

"I haven't been on a date in awhile"

Jael says and Cotton says

"Hell I aint never Jael"

and Jael likes the way he says her name and the way he says he's never been on a date with but her even though she has horse sense and knows that a charmer like Cotton has seen plenty of girls and more though what she don't know is that what Cotton says is true he's never taken a girl on a proper date but her.

25.

Cotton tells Jael to order what she wants for he is a workin man and he knows that money is gone tomorrow and loving it is the root of all evil and it all burns when you die anyhow or some other holy rolling thing so it might as well be gone today. He did not ponder on money thoughts though because when it comes to a girl like Jael with the shape of a fiddle tempting a man like the fruit of good and evil money just don't matter none. Jael orders fried trout and Cotton a steak bygod and he gets a beer not just any beer but the champagne beer that is his most favorite and he makes Jael order real champagne the blonde bubbly though she says it is too fancy she can tell he don't give a good goddamn and like any woman she likes it when a good man bosses her and she don't have to worry none and I suppose this is on account of women havin some of men's rib in em. Cotton thinks she looks mighty sexy in his t shirt turned wet from her bathing suit in all the right places and eatin her trout like a real lady and he knows his manners aint good though he tries bygod and he says

"Sorry bout my eti-quette it aint what it should be"

though he's never apologized about it before and maybe he shoulda but all them other girls he's known before didn't matter all that hell of a much to make you want to hold a fork right no disrespect to them and Cotton would mean no disrespect to them that is just the truth and Jael goes

"I don't care about that Cotton"

and it's real sweet of her to say so like the champagne she is sipping. They sit and eat and talk and talk and laugh and they have a good old time high on the hog and Cotton may even talk a bit too much about his past a little and tell this girl how he is from Oklahoma even bygod and how he has wandered for many years like a miner prophet minor though his profitin skills may be and she laughs and asks him about his family but he don't want to talk about it none not that he's bein rude and Jael knows this but he just does not want to talk about it all the same hell this is their first date and she is right polite about it and drops the subject. Cotton aint never told a girl about his past sides what they already know about him but there is somethin about this blue eyed dark haired girl across from him that makes him drops his dukes a bit and it feels good not to have to be so all fire bowed up. He likes this girl and it doesn't hurt no one for him to tell just a bit about bein an Okie and all but he sorta wonders if it is the right thing but truth be told he don't know his own right from his own wrong when he talks to this girl which is the only kind he follows.

At the Lodge there is a band playin and the bull and the belle do some rug cutting in their crazy get ups and they have a gay ol time and Cotton can dance not just square and Jael wants to know where he learns to dance like that and he said

"If I told ya I'd hafta kill ya"

as they whirl across the floor then Jael gets up and takes the man in the band's guitar and she bygod plays it and Cotton slaps his thigh and calls

"Whooooooeeeeee"

for she plays good and there aint one damn thing he has seen that she can't do and her bare legs are comin out from under the guitar all sexylike and Cotton feels for sure he might be in love if ever he was. Then she bosses the band around and they play and she play n sings a song and Cotton hears her sing and his heart gets all swoll up or maybe just his throat but it's a feelin just the same. Jael woman's voice is real good kinda low and sexy and smooth and bydamn she is amazing from her head down to her hips to her toes to her mug making swimsuit sewing breakfast cooking landscape painting guitar playing sexy singing self.

After the dancing and singing they drink the place into closin time just like they did the bowling alley and by now their clothes are dry and they stumble laughing out into the warm summer Blackfeet wind and Cotton says

"I'll drive you long as your daddy aint gonna shoot my ass"

and Jael says

"He won't bygod"

and Cotton says

"Damn girl you shoulda been the one in the family that went out to Hollywood you're amazing. Have y'ever thought about bustin out"

and Jael laughs like it aint no thing but it is and says

"No I guess not. I always thought I'd stay here. I don't need to go anywhere to be somebody"

and hell this hits our Cotton right in the chest like a bird that flies into a window but can't get inside.

They get to Cotton's Forest Service truck but who should be out in the dark by the truck bygod but that jackass Terry the kid but he aint no dummy no more in matters of Cotton for he aint on his feet he is in his truck with the window rolled down and the engine arunnin and someone is with him and he shouts out

"Hey lovebirds"

and Jael goes all stifflike and Cotton can tell she is scared and he wonders what kind of man Terry must be to make Jael flinch so for she aint the flinching kind but as soon as he wonders this he knows. Cotton don't get his feathers ruffled easy and he knows he can take whatever Terry can dish out so he hollers

"Hey knobhead why ya flappin your gums aint you

sposed to be at home in bed with your momma"

and Jael has never heard such a thing so she does a surprised laugh like she doesn't even want to but she can't help it and Terry's head about explodes for Cotton has seen a man's head explode and Terry's is gettin pretty damn close. Terry kid revs his engine like he is going to drive toward them and Cotton moves Jael toward the truck and Terry shouts

"Hey Cotton she isn't going to be walking down any aisle in white"

and Cotton knows that any man that says that about a woman is the one that put her in the black in the first place so he shouts

"Neither did your momma"

and Terry's head explodes not for real of course just by this I mean he gets mighty angry and snaps and he steps on the gas and roars his truck toward Cotton and Jael and Cotton picks up Jael and puts her in the back of his truck then stands right in front of the Terry truck that is driving toward him he just stands there.

What Terry and Jael don't know though I am tellin you this is that Cotton is the wrong man to play chicken with for once he played a game of chicken with a man who said Cotton had stole his wife so they got two cars though Cotton had long since lost his driving license and drove them real fast at one another dead on and neither one would swerve and they ended up wrecking the cars head on like two jackhammers headbutting and Cotton busted his head on the steering wheel but his head is so mule hard bygod he broke the steering wheel right back. Cotton got out of the wreckedup smash car and dragged the other man out of his wreckedup smash car and Cotton shook the man's hand and he said

"Any man that wants a woman that bad oughtta have her bygod"

so he let the man and his wife be and I hear they are still married and happy in Northern California by the Ocean bygod. I say all this to say that as Terry was plannin on runnin Cotton over Cotton was damned if he was budging he would rather take a chance on God and his own body and see what was left in his hand after his hand was played but then he hears Jael holler at him and he thinks what a goddamn silly way to go so just as he is about to get hit by this truck he steps to the side just like he stepped to the side on Terry in that boxing match and he yells a filthy word like he did that day in the boxing match that Jael can't quite make out in the truck roar. He steps to the side and the truck flies past and the mirror nicks him and he is full of mad mule bull rush rage so as the bed of the truck goes by him he throws his shoulder and all his weight into the side of the truck bed so hard that I swear and Jael will say this too and hell even Terry will admit it dammit that the truck bed was dented clean in and the truck bounced and shifted to the side so hard a good coupla feet from Cotton's body blow that it fishtailed and Terry ran off the road and into tree with a great wrecking ball crash. Jael shouts after Cotton but he runs to the wrecked truck and the last time he played chicken he pulled a man out of a wreck to shake his hand but this time he goes to pull a man out of a wreck to beat him to death and Jael is very afraid for she does not want any more trouble for Cotton or herself being as how his strings hum in her curvy body. Cotton bout rips the truck door off its hinges and he punches Terry who is still seeing stars from the collison about the face and head and neck and back then Cotton begins to drag him out as he is hitting him and hollerin on him but then the man who is with Terry in the truck says

"That'll be enough"

and though the man's voice is warbly scared like a yellow warbler bird Cotton knows he means it by the way he says it so Cotton looks up and the reason this man means it is that he has a gun and he is pointing it right at Cotton and Cotton sees that it is the same jackass he beat senseless and left in the tree as a bar brawl crucifix that night at the grange and Cotton says

"Well I'll be a hornswoggled monkey's uncle"

26.

Once when Cotton and his baby brother was just little they were workin on a pig farm to help support their momma cause their daddy was no good and they were busting it real hard though they were but ten and eight years old apiece. They were workin with a mess of goddamn pigs that were bigger'n them and the owner of the farm had said to Cotton when Cotton came knockin for a job

"You sure you can handle these animals bein how small y'all are?"

and Cotton says

"Just try us mister"

and that mister did try them and he grew real fond of them Kingfisher boys and kept havin em come on back to labor and he called Cotton his little smart ass and the boys thought it was funny and he taught the boys how to cuss though they knew it from their daddy but the pig farmer made it fun. It was the filthiest job one could ever have for the pigstench from the pigsmanure gets into your clothes and even your skin and you cannot wash that goddang stench off of you but Cotton and his brother were makin dough so they didn't care none.

One time on the pig farm a great sow broke her back she was so fat and she could walk no more after that and she was no good to the farm nor anyone else alive so they had to drag her out to pasture but she was so heavy they had to tow her by her hind legs behind a horse out of the pen where she was kept.

The farmer gave Cotton's little brother a rifle for he knew Cotton hunted bear with a switch which is to say he was tough and he was teaching Cotton's brother to be tough too though none needed to teach a brother of Cotton Kingfisher's to be tough bygod but the farmer wasn't thinking about this so he handed the rifle to Cotton's little brother and says

"Shoot er right between the eyes son"

and then he left the boys alone with the broke back sow and Cotton's little brother stood there lookin down at the poor momma pig with lil beady eyes and it seemed she was staring up at him and askin him not to shoot her and Cotton's little brother thought of his momma like Cotton does now and he stood there for a long while lookin down at that pig for he could not kill her. They stood there for a piece and Cotton knew that the man would be back to butcher and gut the pig after it was dead so Cotton takes the rifle from his little brother and says

"I'll do it bygod"

and he takes the gun and he aims it at the pig's head right between the eyes just like the farmer man told his little brother to do and he sees the pig looking up at him with those beady lil eyes and he pulls the trigger and kills the pig dead and his little brother flinches and the shot echoes through the trees and crows are cawcussin at the noise and Cotton looks over and his baby brother is cryin and Cotton puts his arm around him and they go.

I tell you this to tell you that Cotton thought of this as he has Terry by the scruff and the truck is jammed into a pine tree and the man who Cotton had left as a bar brawl crucifix that night at the grange is pointing a gun on Cotton with shaking hands and eyes. Cotton thinks about the pig he killed a long while ago for his baby brother and he misses his brother and he wonders whatever came of him and he wonders what he is doing here with a man in his hand and a gun in his face and a girl callin out his name. When he comes to he hears the man yelling at him to drop Terry and Cotton knows that when there are guns it has gone too far and not because he is scared but because he has faced guns before and he's never cared for them he has always used his fists and he feels like it is cheating even in War not that he talks about War but he always felt it was cheating but he liked cheating better than dyin so he has used a gun himself but never cared for them.

"I see how it is" he says to the man with the gun "you can't finish your bygod business by your own damn self and neither can this pissant hissy fit kid" and the man who has the gun is scared shitless as they say for he has never heard such talk from a man with a gun in his face and his hand is shaking so bad he doesn't know if he can hit the broad side of a barn the barn bein a mulekick Okie hellraiser cuss.

"Put him down mister or I'll shoot I swear I will"

the man with the gun says almost like he's beggin and Cotton can hear Jael calling him and he feels the blood running out of his head so he takes Terry real roughlike and throws him into the back of the truck and says to the man with the gun

"Get the hell outta here you sonsofbitches"

and the man who is still holding the gun real shakylike manages to back the truck out of the tree and drive it back to Stumptown rattling and coughing all the way. Cotton heads back to his truck and he feels a little off kilter for thinking on that story of his brother and the broke back sow dead pig and guns and men and Jael is settin up in the bed of his truck looking pretty but a little sadlike like a far off star twinkling that you cannot grab no matter how high up you reach and people have come out of the lodge though it is late and Jael still has his white t shirt on and he hefts her down outta the truck and they don't say nothing as they head back to Stumptown to drop Jael off. Cotton tries to say something but he don't got nothin to say so he just smokes and he can tell Jael is looking out the window at the big dark pines and thinking big dark thoughts.

Cotton drops Jael off at her and her daddy's house and says goodnight but it is real quietlike and Cotton feels quiet himself and I will tell you why they are both quiet it is both of them are starting to think that they may apiece not be the best thing for one another on account of all the trouble and trouble is fine with Cotton but trouble with guns and girls is another kind of trouble all together bygod and we all know it and so does Cotton. Only after Cotton leaves and is deep thinking dark sky pine thoughts that he remembers Jael is still wearin his t shirt but she didn't forget she didn't tell him on purpose when they say goodnight and she sleeps in that t shirt and nothin else that night though she thinks that they may apiece not be the best thing for one another on account of all the trouble.

Cotton tells Jacob Two Calves all about the chicken wreck gun brawl on Monday when they are out in the forest and Jacob feels a deep dark crow flapping in him at the talk of a gun being pointed by a man at another man both whites too for godssakes and he knows that he aint seen it all just yet and sho nuff while Two Calves was thinking of another kind of trouble a goddang bear wanders right upon them in the woods where they are workin and they are too far from the truck to make it back and all they got is a couple of pulaskis and a shovel and some smokes. When Cotton sees the bear he looks up at it then lights a cigarette like it aint nothin though it is bygod and the bear gets up on his hindlegs and he is a big goddamn bear maybe not a grizzly but goddamn close enough even Two Calves thinks so and that old bar smells Cotton's cigarette smoke and this is what Cotton wanted though he never said a word to the bear or Jacob or God about it. Jacob Two Calves lays on the ground so as not to rile the bear but Cotton don't he just stands there smokin like it is his goddang forest though he and the bear both know it aint he still acts it. The bear rares up and looks at Cotton and stands there for a minute trying to look all impressivelike but he sees Cotton aint buyin it so he gets back down on all fours and get this I swear to you bygod and so will Jacob Two Calves to this day that the bear walks right on by Cotton so close that Cotton reaches out his hand and touches it hairy back and the bear does not even care like Cotton is just another animal that he don't need to tussle with. It was such a sight that Jacob Two Calves nearly soils himself and after the bear is gone Cotton laughs though Jacob doesn't know why but he laughs and shakes his rattler necklace and Jacob Two Calves has never seen a man touch a bear though he is an Indian and he believes it is a sign whether good or bad he does not know but a sign just the same. What Jacob Two Calves does not know but I do and you have probably heard this too is about how Cotton wrestled a bear in the mountains of Washington and he beat that bear's ass and after he beat it the bear came and nuzzled him and they got along fine after that and when men say he hunts bear with a switch they mean Cotton.

Cotton tries to keep yonder woman Jael off his mind but he doesn't do a whole helluva good job there for he can't get her and her wet bathing suit and her deer roamin jawline out of the back of his eyelids and it plays over and over like a picture on the big screen and he forgets what he is doing and this aint like him. After the gun ruckus Cotton goes back to the cabin and packs his rucksack and lays it by the door and Jacob Two Calves sees this but he don't say nothing and Cotton never says he is leaving but I will tell you what Jacob knew though Cotton did not say is that Cotton is thinking it is about time to be headin on when men draw down on each other over a goddamn girl but on the other hand I will tell you this though Cotton didn't say it either but he thought it is he just can't seem to leave. He knows he should bygod for a storm is brewing like a hot pot of joe about to boil over but every time he thinks of that Jael girl he don't want to go nowhere and he thinks nuts to Terry and his goons he has not ever been chased off and he will never especially when there is such a pretty girl to dance with and he aint even kissed her yet bygod.

After it all Cotton does not hear from the girl for days so he heads into town to look after her with Jacob Two Calves and Mason's words ringing in his ears like a bull's club upside a boxcar

"Don't get into trouble"

but he don't plan to he just wants to see the girl and see if she still has his t shirt that is all for a man needs his shirt don't he so I will be damned if Cotton doesn't go straight to the police captain's house which is Jael's house and as he gets out of his truck the captain meets him at the door in his shirtsleeves and says

"Get going you ornery cuss she can't see you"

and the captain is speakin Cotton's language now and Cotton likes it though he is telling him to get so he says

"Good afternoon Capn"

but the captain shakes his head as if he just wishes Cotton had never been born or at least come to the meaty part of Montana and says

"Goddamnit haven't you done enough"

and by the way he says this Cotton knows something is wrong so he hollers Jael's name at the house but there aint no answer back from the house.

27.

"You've caused a whole heap of trouble for this town and my daughter" the captain goes on "and she's got a black eye and more from getting hassled on account of you so please Jesus just get out of town"

but Cotton barely hears the last part for he sees Jael pushing past her daddy to the porch wearing an apron covered all in flour and her daddy captain Carter throws his hands in the air like he is givin up bygod and goes back on into the house. Cotton can see plain as the crooked nose upon his own face that Jael has a black eye like she put her make up on drunk like Cotton has seen before but he knows this girl has never put her makeup on drunk and she sees him and she says

"What's all the hollering about"

though she bygod knows and Cotton hollers

"Who did it"

though he bygod knows and Jael she does something real sweetllike but it is wrong as well she says

205

"Who did what"

being that she is trying to keep Cotton out of trouble
for she knows if he knows Terry belted her that he
will belt Terry til he's dead and then he will be run
outta town on a rail or worse thrown in prison or
worse dead.

"Now don't give me that bygod I can see that shiner"

Cotton hollers for he sees his momma standing
there busted all up with a bleeding trickle smiling
like nothing happened.

Jael reached her hand up to her face and says

"You think you're the only one who gets into
brawls?"

and this makes Cotton angrier n a wet hen in a
hornet's nest for she is deliberately not telling him
what happened and joking about it besides and that
aint funny bygod so he points at Jael and says

"Now you're pissing me off"

and Jael shouts

"Don't you get fresh with me Cotton Kingfisher!"

but she knows the jig is up and she knows and there
is nothing she can do to stop Cotton from going all
Old Testament on Terry's ass and even though she
would like nothing better than fire and brimstone to
rain down upon Terry's bygod head she don't want
Cotton to get hurt or dead or in jail for her strings
hum for him.

"This is what Terry wants is to get you into trouble"

she says and now she aint jokin now she is pleading and he says

"Well then he did the right thing bygod where is he"

and she says

"They are setting up a trap for you so just stay away from them. Go and talk to Mason and figure what to do but don't go alone"

"Like hell I won't"

Cotton growls and he goes and hops on back into his truck with Jael shouting for cooler heads to prevail and her daddy just shakin his head but Cotton drives hard and he sees his momma standing there smiling all skittishlike smoothin out her dress with blood coming from her nose and lip like nothing has happened though he can see with his own two eyes it has just like the black eye writ upon Jael's face.

Cotton goes lookin for Terry the shit kid to kick the shit out of him all around Stumptown up and down the town but Terry aint no dummy and he has hid somewheres and when Cotton goes into the Dog Leg Carl tells him so and Cotton can tell Carl is tellin the truth by the whites of his eyes but he don't like Carl no more than he likes Terry on account of how Carl fired Jael over Cotton winning the brawl and he tells Carl

"Gimme a goddamn beer"

so Carl goddamn does though he don't goddamn

wanna and Cotton slaps some change on the bar then drains the longneck in one pull while all the roughnecks stand about nervouslike and try to make their way to the door and when Cotton is done with the beer he takes the empty bottle and throws it real hard at the liquor counter behind the bar where it explodes and bottles come crashing down and Carl drops to the floor and Cotton hollers

"and that goes for the rest of all y'all as well if you hide that goddamn kid"

then storms out of the Dog Leg and the men feel funny way deep down in their loins and not in a good way for they have never seen a man throw an empty beer bottle just to break up good liquor like that whether he be angry or not.

Cotton goes out and bird dogs it around the town but he cannot shake anyone down and he sees no sign of Terry nor his gang then he gets to thinking that he has been gone from the cabin at the park far too long and what if Terry has come there and so he heads back fast and makes it back to the cabin but they have already been there and Jacob Two Calves is laying on the floor covered in whiskey and blood and Cotton knows they beat him and soaked him in whiskey to make it look like he was a drunk injun to get him fired. Cotton carries Jacob to the truck and lays him gentle in the back telling him it'll be alright kid Cotton is here but Jacob don't respond none just his head rolls about so Cotton takes him into Stumptown to the hospital and they say that there is a medical facility on the rez take him there and Cotton says he will kill them all one by one if they don't take his injun friend and so they do take him bygod. Cotton knows now that he has never stayed long enough nor cared enough to have his enemies go after the people he likes and it makes him mean angry like he wants to kill somebody and he knows he can't leave now for the wolves are picking off the weak to get to the bull and if it is the bull they want bygod they can have him and his whole rack in their bellies. So Cotton tries to figure where Terry is hidin and he thinks long and hard but he can't yet figure so he goes back to the cabin and drinks and smokes angry like the Bible says you shouldn't and lays on his bed and he passes out heavy angry sometime during the night without his most favorite Indian blanket or securing the door.

Cotton dreams about hell or a rough approximation thereof for it is hot and exploding like a damn Fourth of July going off and he knows it's all goin to hell and he can't fight it fightin only makes it worse. In this dream Ol Scratch or Ol Blickey as his daddy called him is sittin on Cotton's chest and breathing sulphur into his lungs and Cotton has wrestled with the devil before but he's always beat him but in his dream he can't. Then he wakes up and it is still hot and smoky and hard to breathe and bygod it aint no dream the cabin is on fire and hotter n Old Blickey's and Cotton knows them Terry's greaseballs have set it ablaze to frame him or kill him or both so he grabs his rucksack there by the door and hurtles out the door and he lays on the ground hackin and coughin on the blacklung phlegm watching the cabin burn and suddenly he gets hit with bats and axe handles and shovels and he swears even a crowbar and Terry and his gang are upon him and they are shouting for him to get out of town and he is groggy and heatstroked and coughin but in mule buck rage he manages to rush an attacker and break the thug's leg at the knee and grab a man's privates and twist em near plumb off as the man screams and snap a man's wrist and break some ribs and noses and jaws but the men were prepared the best they could be and they sling chains around his legs though he manages to break a couple of faces with the chains he goes down and he can't get up and he feels heatstroked hard and they hit him in the head over and over and he breaks more bones and he hears Terry screaming

"Good God man give up"

but this just makes him madder'n a cockfight rooster and makes him fight harder but the harder he fights the more colors he sees before his eyes like the lightnin bugs back home that is one of the things he misses out West and he hears dings and zingers and finally the whooshing devil laugh of the Tillamook burn that took his friend and he grabs an attacker like he grabbed that man from out the burning log that fell upon him in Tillamook and he hears a whoosh and a crack and it all goes big sky black.

Cotton sees and hears wrens and robins and barn swallows about his head circlin round and around tweeting like lil sonsofbitches and he feels dancers kissing on him all over and he hears the train and he opens his eyes and bygod it is a train. He sits up and he is covered in dry blood crust and bruises and welts and he sees that he and his bag have been thrown out at the Stumptown rails at the end of town and Terry and his boys have run him out of town and they want him to take the train out. Cotton feels dizzy sick in his head and heart so he lays his head on his pack and fumbles in his pack and gets his canteen and he drinks some water and it makes him feel a bit better but not much for he has never been beat and now he is beat and there is no way to change it. He lays there next to the tracks of the Empire Builder line that heads out East and he feels like death warmed over and all sensitivelike like the earth has finally done it it has killed him or close enough that he wishes he was dead for he has been beat and he don't have a place to go and he thought this here meaty part of big sky The Land Where the World Began was really for him and shit on a stick it aint and nothing is for him why did he think it would be this is what he thought. He sees the blood on his clothes and the blood on his momma's face and on his daddy's head after he guitar beat him and he thinks of the blood of the lamb and his momma and brother and sisters and he knows he is being punished for runnin away and leaving his family like that bygod. He wants to cry but I don't know if I have told you this he does not know how so he doesn't cry he just lays there and waits for a train to come because he is bygod done and he let himself pretend to be somethin he is not and what he was pretending that he is not is that he was a keeper. He wonders what that beautiful big sky girl could ever see in his broke up face and broke down spirit and he has just caused her lots of trouble and damn it is time to be movin on besides who needs all this goddamn trouble. Cotton is laying near the Stumptown tracks thinking sad earth beatin him thoughts when someone comes up to where he is laying and he looks up and bygod where has he been it is the minister of the presbeterius church and Cotton is in no mood to say here or nothin at all so he is quiet.

"Good Lord" the minister says "what did they do to you?"

and Cotton says

"Who gives a damn I'll be outta your hair as soon as another train comes"

and the preacher does somethin real sweetlike he kneels down next to Cotton in the gravel and says

"I thought you might be trouble but I see the trouble is here in town"

and Cotton appreciates this but it don't make a shit bit a difference now does it and he growls

"Leave me alone preach the town got what it wanted I'm leavin off so leave off yourself"

and the minister says

"Who said anything about leaving?"

and Cotton looks at him for this is the very thing Fred Mason said to him that one day he tried to take off his government green shirt after the captain called Mason about Cotton beating Terry.

"Don't let those boys treat you like this"

the minister goes on.

"I thought Jesus said to turn the other cheek"

Cotton smartass sasses and the minister says

"Well the last time I checked you sure as hell aren't Jesus"

and Cotton wants to laugh but it hurts too much and he thinks he might of misjudged this minister so he says

"What about makin peace with the earth"

and the minister says

"I said to make peace with the earth but I didn't mean to give up. There isn't ever any peace without a war"

and Cotton knows he has misjudged this little damn Holy man who is always tryin to sneak up on him and he don't feel so bygod hot so he passes out.

28.

When Cotton wakes up he sees the minister has left him some food out of the church food bank barrel goddamn canned beans but food just the same and Cotton eats them cold beans from the can and waits for a train then he sees someone else coming up on him and it is Fred Mason his boss friend and Cotton don't want Mason to see him like this so he covers himself in his blanket and rolls over as he is too broke up to walk away.

"Cotton" Mason hollers "Come on man I heard about what happened to you and Jacob. Jael came to me and said they were planning on getting you but I was too late. I'm sorry friend I really am. Now come on Elsa has a bed made up for you and some food and the kids are worried. Come on home with me and rest up."

"No"

Cotton says through his blanket on his head.

"Why the hell not you stubborn Bull"

215

"Cause the earth don't want me here and when the earth don't want ya you gotta get to rollin"

"What?" Fred Mason says all angrylike "I have never heard you talk like that before you goddamn sonofabitch stop being a baby and get up and get with us. There's a fire up North and we need you Terry doesn't know enough to handle it alone"

and when Fred says the name Terry Cotton gets angry that his friend Fred Mason still has Terry on the fire crew though he is a man and he knows this is just the way it is with men whether good or bad.

"I'm leavin so forget about me"

Cotton says and Mason gets angry and hollers

"Are you really just going to leave us like that? What if the forest burns down"

and Cotton says

"Let er burn"

and Fred Mason says

"Damn you then you big sonofabitch I thought more of you than that"

and he drops a picnic basket with food that Elsa has made for Cotton and he turns and goes for there is a fire and he fears it might get worse before it gets better even worse since Terry is leadin the crew and he feels sick about his friend the Bull Cotton Kingfisher being broke down like that it was worse than he thought. After Mason goes Cotton can eat some food so he does he eats Elsa Mason's cold fried chicken and homemade bread and he wonders how many days he has been out and he thinks it is several but he can't tell. He eats and sleeps and hears a train go by in his sleep but he can't wake up for it and the next day someone comes to see him and bygod it is big sky woman Jael but he sits like a hobo Indian chief who has lost his tribe and lands with his Indian blanket around his shoulders not lookin up at the girl. Jael kneels down next to him and he won't look at her and she gets awful sad to see him so and still bloody and muddy and all and she whispers

"Are you ok?"

and he says

"Do I look ok to ya?"

and she has to admit that he does not indeed look ok to her for he has lost the fire in his belly as well as his body.

"I am sorry Cotton" she says "I am sorry this happened to you"

and he don't want to talk about it or hear pity from a beautiful girl especially a beauty mark girl he is so fond of for Cotton is built of flesh and blood and bone and gristle held together with pride bygod so he turns his head a bit away from her and says

"I don't need you to feel sorry for me and I won't cause no more trouble cause I'm leavin"

and she says

"After all this you are just giving up?"

and he gets angry when she says this and he says

"I aint never give up missy"

but he still won't look at her and she goes on

"You always give up you move from place to place every time it gets too hard for you! I thought that The Land Where the World Began and all was more than that and I thought you would lick Terry clean into the ground before you would just give up on this place or me"

and she says three things that go in like bullets and come out the other side and one is that he always gives up and the other is that he's give up on The Land Where the World Began and another thing that hurts is the third thing that he gave up on her and this hurts the worst so bad that he does not even have an answer and they are both quiet man and woman like Adam and Eve settin sad outside the garden after God booted them out and the Blackfeet wind picks up off the mountains like that night outside the bowling alley under the big sky but in its coolness is fire. Cotton sits there like a goddang hobo injun chief with his blanket round his shoulders staring at nothin just not at Jael and Jael is squat right down next to him and she goes

"You can't quit now Cotton Kingfisher"

and Cotton growls

"I aint never quit it's just the gettin is good and you gotta get when it is" and Jael says

"You are a coward"

and she is tryin to make ol Cotton mad and hell if she didn't for he turns to her and says

"You're an ornery little shit don't take that tone with me"

"See you haven't lost the fire in your belly yet so get up and use it bygod"

Jael says all riled uplike for she is not used to seeing Cotton broke down and she don't like it and she wished he weren't broke for when a man is broke it weighs down a woman's soul for she knows she can't fix it but it still hurts her in the ribs.

"You once told me to put it all on you and I did dammit and now you are just taking it all back and I never would have put it all on you if I had known you weren't worth betting on"

then she hands Cotton a wad of something and it is the goddamn cash she won in the match and she says

"I haven't spent any of it not a red cent and I don't want it because it isn't right to take money that you didn't win so you take it you stubborn ass"

and Cotton growls

"Leave off you won that fair and square just like I won the fight"

for it makes him powerful angry to hear a woman

talk to him so and they aint never for he is an ornery cuss though he has never hit a woman bygod but they would never want to tempt him to in the first place is what I am saying to you. Jael just keeps her hand out and sticks it in Cotton's face and he gets angry and grabs her wrist and he wonders at it for it is so thinlike that he could break it like a chicken bone though she is a hearty woman and he says

"Get that trash outta my face"

and Jael says

"Are you going to black my other eye"

and this hurts Cotton like nothin aint ever hurt him before like a knife gash he had once but worse for no knife cuts so deep as a woman sayin something like that to a man we all know it bygod so let's not pretend it aint so. I am not tellin no fairy tell I am telling a real bygod story and this part is as real as me or you sittin here listening to or telling this tale. Cotton sees his momma's dog sad worn dress eyes that are drowned when Jael says this and he also sees Jael's eyes and they are fire fightin eyes flashing like Old Man sun and she is beat up like his momma from her black eye but she aint broke like his momma and he lets go of her wrist and she goes and throws the cash on him and stands and says

"Go on get then"

and Cotton wants to holler filthy words at her like the crows are always doin to him but he can't he can't even make a sound he just sits there watching Jael walk off from the railroad tracks and a train is comin in bygod and she disappears behind the many colored cars like Joseph's coat his daddy give him and the train pulls in and it is the big G as the hobos called it and it is goin out East and none of the rail workers will stop Cotton from getting on to go East to finally shake the blood of the West off himself for once and for good and Cotton realizes that he is on the hump the hump being the Continental Divide and he is right smack dab in the middle of comin or goin either way.

29.

When Cotton went to leave his homestead home that time for good after braining his daddy with the guitar I will tell you though no one knows this yet but I am tellin you for people learned it later is that Cotton came down from the tree and went to his baby brother who was sleeping in the shanty and he woke him up and he whispers

"Come on Comanche let's light on outta this place"

and his baby brother was asleep but he woke up and he was but ten or eleven I think and he didn't have quite the cuss that Cotton had and as much as he feared his daddy he feared not knowin what was out there worse and he was scared of the dark and snakes and killing broke back sows besides and he looked at Cotton's boy face which looked man hard in the moonlight and he was scared to go so he shook his head and Cotton said

"Come on ya big baby"

and Comanche Kingfisher says

"I can't Cotton I can't"

and Cotton says

"Why are you scared"

and his brother said

"Yes bygod"

and Cotton said

"You don't need to be scared I'll take care of everything"

and his brother knew he probably would bygod but he couldn't shake the fear for he was just a little boy and had a more tender heart than Cotton who took most of the brunt of his daddy's beatings and besides like I told you Cotton always just had a fire in his belly from the time he came outta the womb and he did indeed kick his momma and the woman delivering him so hard that they were hurt and his little brother Comanche never kicked no one. Now Cotton could see his baby brother was backin out on him for they had always said they would one day run away together and here Cotton had gathered his marbles to do so and his baby brother was just lying there sweatin in the Oklahoma cicada mule hot night saying no I won't go and Cotton felt mighty sad in his guts like he'd a stomach ache from too much pork that the pig farm funny boss had give them from the sow with the snap back that Cotton had shot his damn self so he goes on

"I'll take care of ya and better'n daddy ever could any day goddamnit. I can hunt and fish and cook and work and we could ride the rails West and look for injuns real ones not the broke kind and we could live real high on the hog bygod come on ya baby let's go"

and Comanche who may be named after an injun but no one really knows says

"What about the girls"

and Cotton hadn't even thought of this but they are too little to bring so he says

"Well we could come on back for em after we have enough dough"

and Comanche doesn't seem to care for this and Cotton gets angry for Comanche cares about the girls more than him but more than that Cotton feels guilty like lead in his belly for leaving his baby sisters that Comanche can't and Cotton is just a boy but he wonders what is wrong inside him that he could just leave his baby sisters but he can and he will.

"Goddamn you Comanche let's get goin before it gets light"

Cotton says and Comanche shakes his head and Cotton can see in the Oklahoma big heavy moonlight Comanche says no but his eyes are sad not dog sad but sad and Cotton knows for some reason Comanche can't come even if he wants to for he can't leave the land and his momma and sisters and Cotton knows Comanche is a better man than he though he may be a fool. The boys just sit there in the moonlight looking at one another for awhile like this is the last time they will ever see each other and they don't want to forget each other's face though they were in no danger of doin this for they had been through hell together and boys that have been through hell together remember each other always. So they sit and look at one another and Cotton finally hands his brother something and it is a fat load of cash and Comanche whispers

"What in hell is this"

and Cotton says

"Its money we earned that I kept from momma and daddy now you take it and don't say a damn to daddy about it now you hear me Comanche"

and Comanche nods his head to say he does hear and Cotton can see that he does and Cotton goes on

"Now you keep that money and you help momma and the girls with it but don't ever tell daddy he will take it and gamble and whore it away"

and Comanche nods and Cotton goes on

"I'll send word for you when I get settled and y'all can come join me and we can do it together"

and Comanche nods and takes the cash from his big brother and says

"But what about you how will you live without the cash"

and Cotton says

"I took a little for myself but I will earn most of it by bustin it like a mule ok"

and Comanche says

"Ok"

and they sit and look at one another for a piece in the humid moon until someone stirs in the room next door and Cotton stands up and he puts his hand on his baby brother's head and he musses his hair good then he slips out and this is when he sees his momma and she waves at him whether goodbye or stay he still does not know and that was the last he saw his baby brother as well as his momma and all the rest.

The reason I tell you this as you sit there waiting is for to tell you what Cotton was thinkin after Jael left behind the train and as he sits there like a hobo broke down chief with his spirit and body broken and the hole in him bellyaching waiting to ride the train. He thought deep sad lake thoughts and the clang of the train didn't mean nothing to him no more and this made it worse and also the fact that the minister and Mason and even Jael had all said the same thing to him is that he had given up the ghost of tryin. They had visited him like three goddamn spirits telling him he wasn't worth a damn for quittin and Jael had even pity paid him and he could make a fine living off of those winnings damn her for a few months and just take in the rails and America East of the divide. He thinks of his brother in the Oklahoma midnight and he thinks of Jael in the Blackfeet wind riding Going to the Sun

Mountain and he thinks of Fred Mason and his silly mustache and his pretty family and he thinks of the sneaky minister who has a fire in his own holy belly bygod. Cotton sits and the train sets in front of him chuffin and huffin while waiting to head East and Cotton knows he could hop on and forget this goddang place and sky and girl and all if he would just go get on that train. He thinks about his brother Comanche and how Comanche wouldn't leave with him and he thinks of him in the moonlight and he misses him like hell for a man misses a limb when he loses a brother and Cotton didn't just lose a brother he lost him on purpose which is his own damn fault dammit and far worse a hurt. Cotton thinks again on how Jael gave him hell and money and he gets to boiling inside of himself at her bein so ornery to him and also Fred Mason was a real sonofabitch as well but they were right in a way because he knows he is gettin when the gettin is good but maybe the getting being good just means he is beat and goddamn hell fire shit damn shit Cotton aint never been beat and he won't be beat bygod. So when the many color coated train rolls on by Cotton aint sittin on the side of the track in his Indian blanket no more and the train whistle blows as it leaves Stumptown like Cotton's tales upon the wind up into the meaty Montana mountains as it heads out East.

30.

The fire in the Park no one knows what started it for it was not a lightning strike nor camper fire and some folks say it was from the burnt cabin that Cotton and Jacob Two Calves had lived in that Terry and his boys had lit that night though no one at the time knew it was Terry and his boys. Some folks say an ember flew like a lightning bug from that cabin fire begot of ill rage and sailed high up into the mountains to bear a fire. I did not see this for myself and neither did you nor anyone else that would speak of it but if you ever watched an ember up jump a fire and land on the ground you can see how this could happen for embers are like rumors they fly away on the wind and the next thing you know a goddamn forest is burning down and this has happened with a few Cotton train whistle tales like embers burnin down forests which is why I am writing this to set the record straight. But anyhow I have no trouble believing it about the burnt cabin ember lightin up the forest for Terry and his goons were prepared to light it but not to fight it and I imagine Old Man Big Sun musta been powerful angry at Terry and his boys and he was getting back at them for Cotton wasn't doing nothin not even being his ornery ass self he was just being so maybe Old Man was punishing Terry by lighting a blaze from the cabin. Whatever the case an ember caught some trees and lit a blaze and up jumped a mountain and the smoke was in the air in Stumptown and at the lodges and the sun turned blood red even on the rez. It was bad enough that Fred Mason went out to work on it personally from the headquarters and he was about to fire Terry and all his crew though he'd no proof yet they'd beat Jacob and Cotton though he didnt need no proof but he needed men bad so he sent em up into the blaze and he called the military to come help for he feared the worst and he feared for his Park and all its beauty. He left his wife and kids at the lodge at the Park entrance and Elsa and other womenfolk even Jael Carter were getting food and supplies for the men goin in to fight the blaze. No one had time to think or stop they just had to act for a fire does not stop nor think it just acts and it jumps especially when the wind picks up and the Blackfeet wind was ablowin.

Jael and Elsa were putting supplies for the men into trucks at the lodge and Jael hears all of a sudden Elsa go all quietlike then say

"My my sweet Lord will you look at that"

and Jael looks up and who should be comin through the entrance of the Park along the road but goddamn swaggering Cotton Kingfisher bygod worse for the wear windblown and hellbent but striding strong like the world can go to hell and Jael stands up like she is standing to attention and she just stands but her heart it jumps up like a flushed grouse and Cotton is the shotgun and she hears a bang in her ears and her heart got hit by Cotton the shotgun comin back to fight the fire. Elsa puts her hand on Jael's back but Jael can't speak none just stand there watching that goddamn crazy hard as stone drifter come walking back like he aint just had the beating of his life no sir like he aint never been whooped no sir and he aint about to be bygod damn everyone for saying it and Elsa says

"That man is unreal. I knew I liked him no matter how nuts he is"

and Jael doesn't say anything just nods. Cotton keeps on walkin like he owns the park until he is standing in front of Elsa and Jael and he says

"I need a truck which way is the fire"

and the women just stand there looking at him and I will be damned if both their ribs didn't ache at the sight of this grown boy fire bellied won't quit cuss acting like it aint nothin that he is here though he still has blood on his clothes and bruises all about him and his hair is mussed from the tussle he took.

"You need to clean up Cotton"

Elsa says because Jael is still too heart shy to speak and Cotton says

"Goddamnit woman I aint got no time for a bath a fire don't take no bath break"

and Elsa laughs and says

"Go get cleaned up you stubborn cuss you can't go fight a fire looking like a damn hobo. Besides you don't want them boys that beat you up seeing you look like that so do as I say"

and Cotton gets cussed irritated but he obeys momma sister Elsa for she is right and he goes on down to the lake and strips bucknaked bygod except for his rattler necklace that Jacob Two Calves made him he don't even care and he jumps into the ice cold water and it stings and knocks his breath clean out of him but it feels mighty fine like a glacier baptismal and when he comes up for air he sees Jael sitting on the lakeshore waiting for him with a towel. He washes up as best he can and slicks his hair and then he walks out of the lake naked as a jaybird and he don't even give a damn and Jael turns her head and hands him a towel and he dries off and Jael hands him a crisp new uniform and he digs in his rucksack and gets clean drawers and a t shirt and puts these on then the crisp new uniform then Jael finally speaks and she says

"Sit"

and Cotton obeys her he sits on a picnic table and Jael combs his hair right on the part real nice like he likes and she even puts his grease in it and it looks nice and he looks brand new except for the bruises. Jael touches his cheek real softlike when she fixes his hair and it feels mighty nice her cool hands on his bruised up mug and she is telling him with her hand on his cheek that she is glad he came back and that his strings still hum in her body and he knows she is tellin him that so he looks into her

Flathead Lake blue eyes and nods and she nods back and smiles and Cotton knows she is the most pretty woman he has ever seen and she makes his heart hurt.

"Why'd you come back"

she asks when he stands after her combin and he says

"Well everyone said I's beat and I don't ever get beat so I am back. I aint runnin for gettin beat bygod. Also you said that you bet it all on me cause I told you to and you're right I did and we won and I don't ever welch on a bet so here is your money"

and he gives her the money back and goes on

"Now you keep that and when I get back from the fire we can use it together. I aint leavin off on you and The Land Where the World Began bygod this is my place I feel it in my belly and bones Jael and I shouldn't of left you like that"

he says that like he has always wanted to say it to someone anyone then he goes on

"and what kinda man is gonna let a forest burn to the ground especially Old Man's First Forest"

"Not Cotton Kingfisher"

Jael says and he crooked grins at her then he leans in and kisses big sky beauty mark crow hair girl on the neck under her bowline jaw and he is still cold from the lake and she is warm from the big sun so she shivers when he does this.

"I gotta get"

he says and Jael says

"I'll be waiting for you when you come back be safe Cotton"

and he says

"Always am"

with his damn crooked cocksure grin like he's a goddang boy saying he will stay out of trouble knowing he won't.

"Make sure Fred makes it back safe Cotton" Elsa Mason says when Cotton starts for a truck "He isn't quite as resilient as you"

Cotton winks and says

"He'll make it or I won't either"

and this makes the women hope and worry at the same time then he hops into the truck with his rucksack and a pulaski and waves at the womenfolk and heads up towards the flames with Jael and Elsa just watchin and Elsa Mason says

"That man is unreal"

and Jael says

"He really is bygod"

and Elsa laughs and hands Jael a cold bottle of beer.

31.

Now all the men were busting it on the fireline tryin to suppress the surge of the devil's mouth from goin on up into the great forests and turning back into Stumptown for if the fire got too hot and the wind blew too hard then bygod Stumptown would be burnt to nothing but a cinder. Fred Mason had built control lines on the fire and they were trying to clear and backburn a bit so as to kill out the fire's hungry mouth by the time it got to em. All the men were working and sweatin in the hell blaze and Fred was on the radio down at an anchor point they had cleared with some dozers. He was on the radio with some men up higher on the fire when who should come walking up to him bygod but Cotton Kingfisher in a brand new green uniform and his Army Navy rucksack and a Pulaski on his shoulder with his hair all slicked and a cigarette in his mouth and bruises on his face.

"I'll be damned"

Fred Mason shouted so that the man on the other

end of the radio hollered back what but Fred wasn't there no more he was shaking Cotton's hand and clapping him on the back and telling him this fire was mean as a sonofabitch and thank God Cotton was there and Cotton asked Mason if he had all his control lines and backburnin and Fred said yes except for a part he'd not been able to get to in the mountain funnel where there was some old mines and Cotton knows if the winds picks up it will direct that fire right through the mountain funnel and burn the whole kit n caboodle.

"Where's Jacob Two Calves is he still in the hospital we need him on this burn"

Cotton asks for I do not know if you know this but Indians are the best firefighters you can have on a fire for Cotton had fought fires with them bygod for the Forest Service would call them into the fires from tribes in the SouthWest and Fred said

"No he walked out of the hospital and came back to work. He was going to cuss you out like the rest of us but he was needed on the fire and besides I think he knew you'd be back"

"Hell I didn't even know that but that Jacob kid is a real Indian bygod he would know"

so Fred calls Jacob off a crew to join Cotton and when he comes down he is dirty and still bruised and stitched from his beatin but he smiles when he sees his wild white friend for they both look about the same and Cotton says

"I mighta figured I'd find you here"

236

and Jacob shakes his hand and Cotton shakes the rattler on his neck and they both know why and they both are happy to see one another.

"We better bust it like a mule"

Cotton says and Fred agrees and Cotton goes on

"Get who you can and give em lots of water and put em in the trucks let's go"

so they load up and even Fred comes and he's got a radio so they drive aways up the road then hike up high and look down and they see black smoke a mile or so below and the fire looks like hell is openin up. More men come in on the line as they try to clear it and burn it so as when the hellfire hits this burnt out line it will die off and that goddamn Terry and his crew show and Mason says

"They're gone as soon as this is over Cotton"

and Cotton says

"I don't give a good goddamn anyhow they suckerpunched me is the only way they beat me but they can't run me off of The Land Where the World Began so let em work"

and Mason and Jacob Two Calves look at one another and they are not sure if they should be glad or concerned either way about Cotton's response so they just look at each other is all.

Everyone even Mason works like sonsofbitches on the line clearing and picking and burning with Cotton running behind them hollering

"Clear that brush dammit" and "Fell that widow maker that'll burn like a fag" and "Put your back into it this aint pickin in high cotton" and "Bust it like a mule boys" like he is some goddamn sergeant during war time and the men obey him as such and what Fred Mason knows from the men he called in Oregon is that men obeyed Cotton in the Pacific in the War just like they are obeying him now on that fireline and in the War if Cotton said get up you got up and if he said lie down you lied down cause he always went first and he was not scared of shit and he never died so he's probably the man you want to listen to that's just the kinda man he was and I guess it'd be alright for me to tell you about this about the War for Fred already knows it anyhow. Even that chicken shit cheat Terry Clay obeyed Cotton and Cotton could tell he was hell scared of him like he was a Okie ghost comin back from the dead that you just could not bygod kill and Terry was not the first man to think this nor the last. Cotton walks up on Terry and his boys clearing a line and he says to the bar brawl crucifix who held a gun on him

"Do you have your gun with you this time"

and the man don't say nothin but Cotton can tell by his eyes darting like a horsefly on a horse's ass that he aint got that goddamn gun and Cotton says to the gun man and Terry with Terry still having bruises and a split lip from the chicken truck wreck

"Good then when this is all over it's just me n you boys and the mountain"

and no one says anything but Cotton can see the first

chance they get they will light out before Cotton has the chance to scob their knobs and worse.

Now the fire is burning madder n Old Blickeys below them and they stand high on the their line and watch and work some more and Cotton lights a smoke for they have backburned and like the cute poster says be prepared to fight it before you light it well they are so Cotton and Jacob Two Calves smoke in the char with Fred Mason who aint a smoker they all stand together sweatin hellhot and Mason says

"What chance we got"

and Jacob Two Calves says

"The wind is picking up"

"Well we got two backburned lines behind us what next"

and Cotton says

"Let's drive the devil into hell"

meaning work their way down into the fire itself to beat it with clearing lines and Two Calves says

"Let's go"

so they heft on packs and shoulder pulaskis and shovels and brush hooks and saws and head further down the mountain across a creek past an old mine down toward the fire to clear another line all the men go like a goddamn army for they know if they don't stop the fire now that Stumptown aint got a chance in hell. Cotton goes crazy with a saw clearing an anchor point and all the men string along from there like Marines forming a line and they go busting it like a mule with the fire rushing like a river below them then they start to feel the heat coming up and the Blackfeet wind picks up and the big sun disappears behind the fire spirit's smoke signal char ash burn and men put wet shirts on their heads and over their mouths and Cotton is like a fire god hacking and heaving and hollering orders beside Jacob Two Calves and Fred Mason. It's when the wild animals come runnin up past the men up the mountain deer and elk and bighorn sheep and even a goddamn bear and cougar and the crows take to wing cussin at the fire and maybe Cotton and the men fighting it too the ornery black sonofbitches it is when this happens that the men and Cotton know it is time to beat it like hell and Cotton roars louder than the fire

"Get on out follow me goddammit!"

Some men stoke a fire with pokers and some men with their bare damn hands and Cotton is the kind that uses his bare damn hands and come to think of it he is the only man I hear tell of to use his hands but he would reach his hands into a fire and turn a log while squintin against the smoke so he aint scared of fire or heat so when he says to get on out of a fire you get bygod and all the men know this. It turns to chaos when Cotton hollers to get for the fire hit faster in the Blackfeet wind rushing like a river of fire and jumps timber and flares up behind the men before they can run and some of the men are falling down in heatstroke and it is black and

240

hot as hell and the fireline collapses and it is every man for himself but the men pick up others on their shoulders and make their way to who knows where and Mason was by Cotton then he is not and Cotton remembers what Elsa told him about taking care of Fred and he will be damned if he lets Mason die even if Elsa didn't say anything about taking care of him so he runs down into the fire calling for Fred while Jacob Two Calves shouts after him but Cotton does not give a damn.

"Mason ya goddamn idjit"

Cotton hollers as he makes his way through the burning cemetery of trees straight into Old Scratch's gullet

"You are gonna get us all killed"

and he finds Mason passed out from heat and smoke on the black earth so he heaves him on his shoulder and starts running uphill and there is a deer running beside him now and she looks at him out of her eye sidewayslike and Cotton shouts at her

"Run momma run"

and she does bygod and so does he with Mason on his shoulder and they bust it like a mule animal and man together trying to beat the devil fire that is eating away at The Land Where the World Began.

32.

The men on the crew make it back to the creek they crossed comin down thank God all of them Cotton counts them when he makes it to them with Fred on his shoulder but the fire has beat them and is coming up and down for Cotton sees it has jumped their line and is burning back down right on top of them and he knows they are trapped so he shouts

"In the creek"

and all the men get in like he says then he says

"Now out"

and they are confused but Cotton knows the creek will be boiling like the devil's own bath in a minute and he just wanted them all wet so he hollers

"Get into the mineshaft"

for there is an old abandoned mineshaft from back in the day when men used to come out to the West boonies and mine for what they could and dump deposits in the creeks so the men start piling in some dragging others and Mason on Cotton's shoulder and Cotton sets Mason down then he sees Terry running out the mine and on off up the mountain and Cotton runs after him shouting

"You goddamn jackass you'll get yourself killed"

not that he cares about Terry being killed but he aint about to let a man on his crew die like that no sir that is just the kind of man Cotton Kingfisher is bygod and Terry is runnin like a chicken with his head cut off so Cotton tackles him by the legs hard and brings him down and it is almost too hot to stand or breath so he punches Terry good in the body so that a rib cracks and Terry loses his air and Cotton grabs him by the collar and drags him by his scruff on his ass down the mountain and into the mineshaft with the others just as a wall of flame comes up like the fiery furnace the firefighters around fifty of them being Shadrach Meshach and Abednego in their mineshaft furnace.

There is water on the floor of the mine and the men lay in it and they take blankets on Cotton's orders and soak em and Cotton takes his own Indian blanket from his rucksack and soaks it then covers Mason with it as the fire rages outside like they were in a stove and it starts to suck the oxygen out of the shaft and men vomit and shout and curse and Cotton and Jacob Two Calves throw water on the mineshaft timbers near the door as they burst into flame and it is so hot the two of them feel the hair on their hands smolder so they throw water on one another but even the water turns hot and the men swear to this day though no one may believe it that Cotton would shout out the mine entrance like he was shoutin at the fire

"Come on if you can I dare ya come on you devil"

and they thought he'd gone squirrel bit crazy like some of the others the others that panicked for they were unable to breathe proper and they ran to get out though it was sure a way to die they did not care for they were driven fire mad and as the men came swarming at the mineshaft entrance Cotton stood in the middle and beat them men down with his fists like Samson beating Philistines comin out of fox tail flame lit fields and Cotton hollered

"Get back you cottonpickin idjits the next man to try it I'll kill bygod"

until the back of his shirt that was to the open mineshaft entrance caught fire and Two Calves poured water on him and shoved him deeper into the shaft and then the men that hadn't passed out covered themselves in wet shirts and blankets best they could and Cotton lay beside Mason in his wet blanket and Jacob Two Calves lay on the other side of Mason and the fire was rushing roaring raging like it was talkin trash and aimed to kill them all by taking the oxygen with a sucking sound like a dying fish floppin on the shore. Cotton reaches his arm over Mason and Jacob Two Calves grabs Cotton's arm right on back so that they lock arms and stay like this until Cotton sees black big sky black with no stars and he hears Old Man laughin in the fire and he sees colors on the back of his eyelids he aint never seen before and he knows they are all dead it was either out there or in here and at least they'll be able to recover their bodies in here. He thinks on his family and the water drowned homestead sounds nice and cool right about now compared to this hell hot heat and he wishes he could swim like a loon to the bottom of that lake and say goodbye to his momma he would not even mind the dive it would feel nice and cool. He thinks on his family and he wonders for them and knows that the earth has got them taken care of whatever happens and he thinks of Jael and this makes him riled for he never even bygod kissed her on her pretty mouth what a jackass this is what he thinks of in a time like this but no man can account for what he thinks of in his time of dyin and this is what Cotton thinks. He knows that the earth has finally kicked his ass once and for all and he does not even mind he's had a helluva go especially here in the big sky state where the world began and he wonders if this is what the minister means by making peace with the earth just that you don't care if it is beatin you or not and yes he supposes this is what it means and then he can't think no more and all he sees is a black cat's back and the lights go out.

There aint no dancing girls in Heaven just one Jael ridin a big rock candy going to the sun mountain with her black hair falling down her naked back and her hair is the big black sky and her skin is creamy and white like the milky way and her beauty mark is the earth the earth that has beat me but who gives a good damn when this is bein beat seeing Jael riding a mountain smiling whoooeee boy. Stars fall like flashing fireworks and don't make a sound but there is the sound of bullets coming past fast and some explosions like during battle.

When you die in Cotton's way of thinking at least people that done you wrong and you done wrong come back to life and tell you they are sorry and it is ok maybe like a dog eyed momma or a mean stringed daddy or a little Comanche brother or a couple of baby sisters and maybe a lot of men you killed whether for right or wrong reasons those men you killed still stay on your soul like finger smudges on a window but when you die they come back to see you and make their peace with you and you with them. When you die you don't get any bigger you just see how small you really are but it is ok because you feel small and a part of something like a part of a great big circle that is complete. When you die there aint no angels with harps just angels with real pretty voices that sing and sing prettier than a daddy's high Okie voice in the Oklahoma hills and there are no mean strings in em. When you die you don't set up on a cloud playing a dang gold harp you lay by a cool river and the good green earth is warm beneath you and there aint no fires to burn up the forests for the earth is living and it warms itself and the trees are bygod bigger'n anything we have ever seen and men don't need to chop them down for to make houses for everyone sleeps out in the open under the stars like a bunch of bygod hobo children but neither poor nor tired nor thirsty nor hungry. When you die there aint no holes in your soulgut or your body or bones and hell there are no scars upon you either when you die and it feels mighty fine like your story aint even been written yet.

This is what Cotton knows of dyin for he would swear bygod and so would a lot of others that he died that day in that abandoned mineshaft on the mountain with all the others there being fifty or so but if he and the others died they didn't die for long for Cotton woke up with a holler and a breath and he sat up straight pulling Jacob up with him for he and Jacob Two Calves still had their arms locked over Mason and get this it had been so hot that their hands prints were seared upon one another's arms like a tattoo that they still wear with pride a story written on flesh of the white man and the red man burned one color bygod. Cotton staggers up coughing and hacking to beat the band like a black lung miner and the others start to roust and Cotton checks on them and they are all alive bygod even Terry Clay who is layin there lookin up at Cotton and Cotton takes a Pulaski like to cleave his head no one'd know or even care now he could kill him and get away with it for jumping him like that and for beating poor innocent Jacob and burning the cabin and giving Jael a black eye and he looks down upon Terry and sees broke back sow eyes looking up and Mason and Jacob see Cotton do something real sweetlike though it be not like him he hands the handle of the Pulaski to Terry and Terry is confused but he takes the handle and Cotton hauls him up off the ground and maybe a mite rough but Mason and Jacob will be damned that Cotton helped that little shit of a kid Terry off the ground even if a bit roughlike but he did bygod. Cotton takes his pulaski and throws it aside then goes to Mason and he and Two Calves help Mason outside of the mineshaft and to the sight they are about to behold. The sight

248

they behold is a black valley of charred snags like a valley of burnt out ghost trees now just a black bent twisted tree graveyard and though it is the saddest sight to behold Fred Mason shouts as loud as his burnt out lungs will let him

"Whoo boy Cotton Kingfisher you saved our asses!"

and the men cannot believe the sight and that they survived though they are still weak and hacking and their skin red like Jacob Two Calves only not by being a Blood but by being burned like baked taters and they stand together and shake hands and cheer and they shake Cotton's hand and praise him and he lights a cigarette with his arm around Mason still holdin Mason up and he says

"It aint nothin"

though it is and all the men know it is for they would be dead but if not for Cotton and Cotton does feel a mite proud to have the men tell him he saved their lives at that. Jacob Two Calves is looking up towards where they came down and he points and says

"Look"

and they all do look and they see up near where they came down the trees are green and the fire stopped bygod and all the men figure it must of been their lines that saved them and Mason reckons it is on account of Cotton had them do several lines and go to meet the fire down this low but Cotton knows it was God that Old Man and so does Jacob Two Calves and they look at one another and they start to laugh like they have gone goddamn crazy and maybe they have who could blame em but they laugh because Old Man came back maybe for just a day but he came back bygod and maybe he brought back the bison Cotton thinks for he could use a damn bison steak right about now.

33.

The men help each other up the steep to get back to their vehicles and there they find the trucks and dozers and all not burned out a bit for the fire stopped before it reached them and there are also military trucks for the Army arrived and came to see about the men everyone feared were dead but they aint dead Mason tells them there military men for the Bull of the Tillamook Burn has saved them just like he did on the Oregon Coast and in the Pacific during the War bygod I knew I put my money on the right man I kept telling them God I told them all and even Elsa believes me this is what Mason tells them as Jacob Two Calves and Cotton load him on Cotton's Indian blanket into the back of the truck while Army medics look him over.

"I can't figure it" says a military man in charge "but by all accounts your lines saved the forest and the town Cotton Kingfisher and your quick thinking sure as hell saved all the men"

and Cotton says

"Ahhh it aint nothin sir nothin at all"

though he knows it is somethin and so does the military man whose rank I am still not sure about but rank enough that Cotton calls him sir.

The men all head back to the lodge headquarters and they have been gone a long time for they were trapped in the mineshaft for nine hours and everyone thought they were dead and so did they but they weren't and if you do not believe in miracles maybe you will now I sure as hell do after I heard all that and heard that it was true for I have it on a reliable source as they would say in betting and in the papers.

Back at the lodge Cotton and Jacob unload Mason and Elsa runs out and falls on her husband and is kissin n cryin for bygod she thought he was dead and she thought she was widowed with the kids but she wasn't and Cotton stands and watches and he feels happy all over to see such a sight like when this same man and woman were dancing that night at the grange with the mountains for their wallpaper and it all feels right with the earth. Mason tells Elsa that Cotton saved everyone and Elsa starts kissin and cryin on Cotton and she says

"I told you to bring him back alive and you did bygod you did you wonderful man everyone can go to hell I knew Fred was right about you"

and the way sister momma Elsa Mason says this makes Cotton the happiest man on the earth as she kisses him and he laughs with his arms folded over his chest like a charred scarred Paul Bunyan and he feels as he has never before and he just can't explain it though you and I probably could as we watch this all. Of course you may be wonderin where Jael is in all of this and so was I until she came runnin up and she stops and stands and looks at Cotton and says

"You ornery cuss we thought you were all dead"

and he says

"But we aint bygod"

and she says

"Well I know that now you big lug"

and she hugs him with all her might and it is a good bit of might and she does not care that Cotton is like he was burned in a fire his clothes tattered and black and his bare skin red and his right forearm seared with Jacob's palm and fingers like a hand of flame. Cotton puts his nose on Jael's hair and it smells like the sun and flowers and not smoke and he feels happy and dog tired and he thinks of her ridin the mountain when he died and he is goddang glad he came back to life to see her for real and feel and smell her not just angel dream her no matter how pretty in the death dream she was. She looks up at him with her eyes sparkling like big sun lake sparkles and Indian paintbrush freckles on her cheeks and they touch noses then they kiss like real man and woman finally bygod what took so long and they feel a hummin in them like they were made from the same earth and bone and blood and fire to be here together and no one can tear em asunder as they say. Fireworks go off in Cotton's noggin like the Fourth of goddamn July when he kisses his big sky mountain girl for the first time but hell not the last bygod and if the police captain Carter Jael's daddy was there he would have seen that it was a lost cause keeping them two apart any longer and Fred Mason did see it and he didn't give a damn about keepin them apart any longer and Elsa sees it and she never wanted them to keep apart in the first place this is what she has been saying all along bygod. Cotton and Jael kiss for a good while and no one makes em stop and there are a mess of Forest Service men now millin about and they come up and slap Cotton on the back while he kisses Jael and it is a big mess of hootin n hollerin for nothin feels better than to be alive when once you were dead can I get an amen.

Cotton breaks off the kiss at one point and says

"I gotta go finish some business"

and Jael says

"Stay out of trouble"

and Cotton says

"I am trouble"

and grins like a little kid crooked grin who is sayin he is trouble and means it then he goes and stands on the bed of his truck next to where Two Calves is sitting to stay away from all the kissin n cryin and he scans the mess of men comin off the military trucks from the mountain and he sees who he is looking for that goddamn Terry Clay kid who he whipped in the ring fair and square that whooped him back not in a fair fight or by himself or without a gun of course and who Cotton could of killed on the mountain just a bit ago but he didn't for he is a better man than that at least now he is. Cotton sees Terry and he shouts real loud at him and all the men milling about stop and are quiet and Terry looks up at Cotton and he knows he aint seen the end of this yet and he wonders why the earth has it out for him and Cotton points his finger at him and hollers

"Get outta my town"

and Terry skedaddles bygod and I don't mean to say that Terry is the devil though he be a shit or that losing your town to a drifter is easy but each man has to go on his own journey to make peace with the earth and Terry's journey was just beginning for they never saw him in Stumptown again after Cotton set his wandering spirit on Terry and Terry bore it and he wandered like Cain with the marks of Cotton written upon his flesh and I swear no man would touch him for it. Then Cotton gets down off the truck and Jael kisses him heavy and they start dancin though there aint no music and they dance and dance and there is the blow of a whistle from a train and Cotton hears it for it is for him but he don't have to go fetch it he can just listen to it tell his tales longandfar on the rails like mythologies that aren't myth because they are true bygod each and every one. The Big Sky Big Sun Old Man is smilin down on them all and the smoke is clearing and the men are cheering and the mountain girl and the once drifter are dancin and Fred and Elsa Mason are watching and so is Jacob Two Calves and they believe they have never seen such a sight as these two people in love with the mountains as their wallpaper and the earth is peaceful like a big boned gentle bison lay down beside its baby on the plains without worry nor fear.

34.

There are more details after the fire and kissing and crying of course and the tale is never done as long as Cotton is busting it like a mule and he still is and always will be I wager. There was fire mopup to be done on the mountain after the fire and Cotton though he was dead dog beat led the crews with Jacob Two Calves and the military back into the char valley of dead ghost charred snags and they cleaned the mess up themselves bygod because that is just the kind of man he and Jacob are. The military that came in said that the crew of fifty men that Cotton saved led by Cotton and Fred Mason had done the work of a unit three times their size and the men who were there even Terry Clay bygod said it was because of Cotton being like fifty men himself busting it like a mule and running from tree to tree to fell and digging trenches with a pulaski all on his own like he was possessed with something with what the men did not know but he was possessed like he meant it and the others followed his lead as well.

The best part about it all is after the fire and mopup and all the fuss Cotton and Jael get this they got bygod married man and wife at the presbeterius church proper by that sneaky cuss minister with the police captain's consent bein Jael's daddy and all and Cotton asked him proper I tell you bygod and of course he said yes for what could he say to the new town hero for godssakes and Jacob Two Calves and Fred Mason were both best men of course and Elsa Mason was Jael's maid of honor of course and all the men from the fire and the whole town turned out for the wedding then there was a damn dance party afterwards at the grange and Cotton outdanced them all bygod and Jael sang him a song under the big sky that the townsfolk say brought tears to ol Cotton's eyes though he does not know how to cry and Cotton may be angry at me for telling you this but I aint sayin I saw it just that I heard it for it is what the townsfolk said about him getting teared up.

Jael did indeed wear white that day damn that Terry Clay for any woman can wear any color she wants on any damn day of the week especially on her wedding day and Jael made the bygod dress herself to boot and it was mighty impressive even Cotton said so when they danced under the big sky out back of the grange after the wedding this is when Cotton said so about the dress. Some of Jacob's Blood family came down from the rez to the wedding and did a pow wow for Cotton for they had named Jacob Jacob Two Calves Firewalker after his work on the fire and they gave Cotton the same goddamn name and still call him that to this day Cotton Kingfisher

Firewalker and they say he and Jacob are brothers from the fire for the marks on their arms and for the work they done together and this makes Cotton a member of the Blackfeets and I cannot tell you what this means to him for there aint no way to tell about how one lost a family but finds another. These rez Indians of Jacob's came in some traditional garb like Cotton had wanted to see his whole life and they did a dance and it was so beautiful Cotton sat with his wedding dress wearing childbearing switchhip girl on his lap drinking a beer and watching and he couldn't say nothin just watch the dance about Old Man coming down to save two brothers from a fire and it was beautiful everyone that was there said so.

Then even after all this there is the part of the Cotton tale about how Jael had a baby boy just the next year who they named Comanche Two Calves Mason Kingfisher after Cotton's baby brother and Two Calves after Cotton's best friend Jacob Two Calves the Blood Indian and Mason after his best friend boss Fred Mason and the last I heard Cotton is working with Fred Mason at the Park all year long they run it together and Jacob works there too and Jael swaddles the baby in that favorite Cotton Indian blanket that he won from an Indian in a drunken bet then gave back to the Indian and said

"Now who's the Indian giver"

and then the Indian gave it back to him for he won it fair and square. This the very same blanket that covered Fred Mason and saved his life from dehydrated burning in the abandoned mine in the Glacier Burn swaddles lil Comanche Two Calves

Mason Kingfisher Firewalker in his beautiful Montana mountain momma's arms and Cotton is a sweet daddy I hear for he can't stand to see children's flesh get stories writ upon them like his daddy writ upon him so I hear he is a gentle daddy bygod though he does like to wrassle that baby for the baby is a boy and a cuss I hear too like his daddy for when he came out of the womb the lady delivering gave him to Cotton and he kicked Cotton right hard in the goddamn jaw and Cotton laughed and said

"Atta boy"

I guess the apple don't fall too far from the tree now does it and the sometime orchard picker that is Cotton would know it. Cotton takes his little cuss kid down to the presbeterius church bench on the one end of town and bounces him on his knee and they watch the many colored like Joseph's coat his daddy give him train cars comin in but they don't hop em no more and the church minister comes out in front of Cotton then sits down beside him and the baby on the bench and they just talk about the earth and Old Man and life and watch them trains.

The state of Montana gave Cotton some medal for saving the town of Stumptown and Glacier Park and they named the creek before the mine where Cotton saved the men Kingfisher Creek and Jael took that medal and the other medals Cotton earned from the War that he had hid in his rucksack and didn't tell none about she took these medals and hung em in the baby's room which she painted a nice blue with trees and mountains on the wall. She put the medals where the baby could always see how brave his daddy was to bust it like a mule though Cotton don't like the idea of bragging about his medals Jael says for him to just zip his lip for she is displaying them no matter and she does bygod.

I hear as well that Jael is teachin Cotton how to play the guitar proper for though he says he knows how to play he don't know the chords at all and he can't read too well so he can't play that well without knowing chords or changes or words and on that matter Jael is teachin him to read well for a man that can't read is like a man that can't see and that is why I am writing this tale about Cotton Kingfisher for you to be able to see.

Now I will tell you that this tale of Cotton Kingfisher has long been on my mind only just now writ and I wanted to get this train whistle tale down and I did bygod I wanted to get it off of the flesh of Cotton and down on paper so when the body is gone the tale is not if you get my drift. I have been following the tales of Cotton for quite a few years and I thought I would never find the man of many stories but hell I did after this last part I just told you. You may wonder how I came across this train whistle tale of a man myself and bygod so did I come to think of it but it started awhile back during the War when I was serving when I heard of a man in the Uncle Sam's Marines in the Pacific who did the feats of ten men and more. I heard of this wild man he had killed more Japs than any Marine and when the Japs captured him and were leading him back to torture the devil out of him for even they knew who he was the ornery American Leatherneck cuss that wild man I heard of was bound about the wrist and neck by the Japs leading him to torture him but he pulled a bayonet from a Jap's scabbard and stabbed him and the rest is all a blur but this man I heard about who later turned out to be Cotton Kingfisher ended up killing over twenty men with but his bare hands and a Jap bayonet is all though there were guns to be had from those he killed but he didn't give a damn he was so ornery and when they asked him why he didn't use a gun he said

"I aint a cheater"

and this Wildman who was Cotton back then when he said this it made his commanding officers feel funny not in a good way deep down in their loins for they were hard soldiers and had never seen nor heard about the kinda bloodletting Cotton could dish out. Cotton went on to beat the Japs so bad that they surrendered the whole damn island this is what I heard that made me wonder for such a cuss and get to lookin for him and it took me quite a few years after the War but I finally found a trail back to him. A few years after the War I ended up in Oregon working for the Forest Service when I heard the same wildman War stories from men that had been in the War with Cotton and had worked with him on the Tillamook Burn after and the head man up in Oregon was in the War with this mule ox man and said Cotton had saved his life by not only killing those Japs with his bare hands and just a bayonet but by then going and releasing a bunch of American prisoners behind enemy lines and leading them to safety and when Cotton was marching them freed prisoners back to friendly lines a lone Jap came up on em with a rifle and started screaming at them to go on back but Cotton just said

"Go get in bed with your momma"

and that Jap just stood there dumbstruck and watched them all go. But anyhow this man in Oregon had Cotton work with him at the Forest Service after the War bein that Cotton had saved his ass in the War and turns out he was right to do this for on the Tillamook Burn Cotton saved a few others and suffered a terrible burn and they tried to get him to stay on but one day he lit out and left a note that said

"Thankee for your kineness - Cotton K."

and when I saw the writing of this note that the man in Oregon kept in his wallet I knew that it was indeed the man I was looking for since the War and hell even before the War. The tales in the War I heard just gave me hope and the man in Oregon gave me the best truth about the man I had been searchin for and this man I had been searchin for it was Cotton Kingfisher who I guess you should know by now bygod is my big brother for I am Comanche Kingfisher and Cotton is my big brother bygod and we thought he was dead like momma but he aint bygod he is alive and well in Montana and sweet Jesus thank you Lord I am headed to see him to tell him the girls are in California and they are married and have children a bunch apiece and they are happy.

I am goin to the meaty part of Montana to get on at the Forest Service with my brother Cotton to bust it like a mule like our daddy used to say together like we used to when we was at the pig farm and a buncha other places though we were but boys. I am going to Montana to tell him about how I was gone when Fred Mason called the men in Oregon but the next year I was back in Oregon and they told me about the whole thing bygod the Glacier burn and all and I knew of a sudden and I headed out to Montana I just goddamn dropped my Pulaski and ran and I caught the train whistle tales of Cotton I didn't have already on the way. I know these tales are true for I caught them from a man who would bygod know he was some black and some blue some black from fire and some blue from beating and his name was Terry Clay and he was hopping the rails out West to go make peace with the earth and he told these tales of Cotton not angrylike like Cotton had kicked him out of his town and stole his girl and I figure Terry Clay already has a head start on makin peace with the earth just by the way he told those tales.

So I hopped off the rails in Montana just like Cotton did and I am headed into the meaty part of the the big sky country to go see my new nephew namesake and my long lost brother and his beautiful mountain momma wife and to work with him for as long as he will have me for I have missed him so ever since that night he left and there have been times when I was bygod sorry I let him leave without me for I was a coward. I hear from tales that Cotton thinks I am a better man than he but that is a damn lie I want y'all to know for he lit out because he had to or daddy'd a killed him and after he left after busting that guitar over daddy's head daddy never hit one of us again bygod and I don't blame Cotton none and neither do the girls and neither did momma God rest her soul she prayed for him every day after he left and I would serve under that man any day of the week if he and Jacob Two Calves and Fred Mason will have me and I know they will for my boss from Oregon who was in the War with Cotton called em last week and said they have a good man coming which is me and I can't wait to see the look on my Cotton's face when he sees me for though we are men and we haven't seen each other since we were boys we will know each other's faces for boys that have been through hell together never forget each other's faces bygod.

Well I guess I better get gettin while the gettin is good for there is a little Indian boy that just came down to the river to tell me I cannot fish here which is just what I bygod wanted for this boy said he will take me to Indian Father for that will be my first stop on the way to Cotton and The Land Where the World Began. As much as I hate to part with you I got to get to Cotton so here ends up the tales of Cotton Kingfisher my brother though they still go on like the whistle of the train in the wind which you can hear if you listen I tell you. I am off under the big state big sky with Old Man smilin down on us all like a Good Big Daddy not like my and Cotton's old man. I am off to make peace with the earth and bust it like a mule but the best part of all is I don't have to do it alone no more for I have found my brother and we will bust it on the line together in the char smokin looking up at one another from time to time and just smilin at each other for life is good and the earth don't just want us back it wants us to be at peace before it takes us back and Good Big Daddy Old Man comes back and brings the bison with him and wont that make Cotton happy for he could use a bison steak right about now and bygod so could I.

Bust It Like A Mule is Caleb Mannan's fourth novel and first to be published. *Bust It* received rave rejection letters from literary agents all over the United Sates, prompting the author to publish it on his own, with his wife doing all the hard work. In real life, he is a husband, father to four, and businessman. He currently resides in Spokane, Washington with his family, where he is just a few hours' drive from Glacier National Park, The Land Where The World Began.

Made in the USA
Middletown, DE
26 June 2015